Island of Dreams

By

Norma Marie

ISBN: 1-4033-4596-1 (e-book)
ISBN 1-4033-4597-X (Paperback)

Library of Congress Number 2002092721

This book is printed on acid free paper.

Printed in the United States of America
Bloomington, IN

1st Books - rev. 08/09/02

I Dedicate This
Book To My
Daughter-In-Law
Linda

Table of Contents

ordered lunch, Paul began to tell him about Gail, and her problem,

Phil, looked at his friend from medical school and couldn't remember ever seeing him so upset. Paul rambled on saying, "I don't know what to do,....not only is Gail in need of help, ...but I'm afraid Donna will get sick worrying over her."

"O.K. Paul. Let' see if we can get your sister-in-law out of town for a few weeks."

"Great, that was my plan.......now all we need to do is convince Gail of this," replied Paul, with relief in his voice.

"That's easy," explained Phil, "she works at the hospital and I'll see to it personally that she gets a physical and is told to take a few weeks leave."

"Thanks Philip, I owe you one!"

Even as they spoke, Philip could see the strain slowly fading away from his friends face as they started to make plans. "I'll call you, when I have things arranged at the island. Once she's there, she'll have to stay on the island, because my friend......there is only one way off.... and that's with my private boat!" Both men laughed, as they shook hands. Paul, held his friends hand a little longer, and harder, as there eyes met. "Thanks Philip, I won't forget this."

Gail, found herself standing in the doctor's office, not knowing why she had been summoned there. After being examined, she listened to the doctor talk. Then turning in anger, she spoke up, "But Doctor, I cant possibly take time off! I'm fine, and there's so much to be done," pleaded Gail. "Please reconsider.....I'll take more time off....anything!" "No...I'm sorry, Miss Hutton." Then standing, he repeated, "You are not to report back to work after Friday, until I say to. That's an order."

3

Hot tears burned her eyes, and her face was flushed, because she was so furious. "Damn it!! They can't do this to me!" she kept repeating to herself all after-noon, even as she cleaned out her locker. OH Hell, I may as well wash all my uniforms again! Suddenly, she was pulling them off the hangers with such force, that the hangers flew in all directions! Damn!! Why did she have to cry? What was the matter with her? It isn't the end of the world....It's only for two weeks. Wiping away her tears, she headed for the nearest exit, hoping no one would see her leave.

As Gail, got into her red Camero, little did she know that she was being observed, from a third floor window, by three doctor's. "Well, she fell for it! My part is done gentleman," stated Dr. Richard Wild, Philip's colleague.

"Wonderful," replied Paul, with a smile, then he turned to Philip, asking, "What plans were you able to make?"

"Well, there's a patient of mine on the island right now, but he should be gone by the time Gail arrives. He, owns a helicopter, and comes and goes pretty much on his own. There's a small field on the back side of the island, where he usually lands. Bill, my chauffeur, and all around handy - man, will take Gail to the island, then he'll pick her up two weeks later. Your sure she's not afraid to be alone? It can get pretty lonesome, and scary out there all by yourself."

"No...I think she'll love it..........once she gets over being mad at the world. She and Donna, use to fish and camp out as children, besides, Gail has been on her own ever since high school.......then with nurses training, and being in the Navy....I don't think she will have a problem there." Even as Paul spoke, he thought to himself, I hope to God, we're doing the right thing.

That night, sitting in Gail's apartment, Paul, told her of a friend of his that owned a beach house, on an island, where she could spend two weeks. Then he began to describe the beach house to her. "It has a large front- room, with a fireplace, and a well stocked bar. There's a large bath-room, and two big bed-rooms, both with fireplaces. The kitchen is ultra-modern and the refrigerator is well stocked."

"Wait a minute!" cried Gail, "who the hell would let out a place like that to a stranger?....What's the gimmick?"

"There's no gimmick," replied Paul, "By letting trusted friends use the beach house, my friend knows that someone will be looking after his property. That's fair enough. Isn't it?"

"Of course," broke in Donna," if you're afraid to be alone. "........then ... forget it."

"No, I'm not afraid to be alone! I'm use to it."

"Then you'll go?" asked Donna, hopefully.

"Maybe. It still sounds to good to be true. Imagine.....being on an island all alone." Then she smiled, saying, "I always wanted to go skinny-dipping, soooo,.....who knows... maybe I will!"

They all laughed, and Paul, proposed a toast to celebrate Gail's departure to this magical island. Two days later, Gail stepped out of her car, and went down the ramp to the landing, where she had pictured a small boat would be waiting for her. Instead...a sleek cabin cruiser was tied up at the dock. Just then, a tall man, in his thirties called out to her, "Right this way, Miss Hutton. Watch your step."

Paul, passed Bill, the suitcases, also a box stuffed full of tapes and books. Gail carried her fishing pole, and tackle box with her. Once everything was on board, Paul, told Bill, to take good care of Gail. Then he turned and kissed Gail, saying, "Get some rest, and I want to see you tanned, when you return!" Then he laughed and called out, "All over that is!" The two sister's kissed and hugged each other good-bye. Gail, was still smiling as the cruiser pulled away from the dock. Donna waved back, knowing that she would worry about her being alone on the island, even though Paul, and Philip, both agreed, this was for the best.

When they were out of sight of land, Bill, told Gail to go below and to put on another sweater, also the rain slicker that was hanging on a hook, as the wind was picking up and the sea was going to get rough.

Once below deck, it dawned on Gail just what an adventure he had taken on. Suddenly she had a queer feeling in the pit of her stomach, and she didn't know if it was from the motion of the boat, or that she was just plain scared. Or both! Gail, made coffee and brought a mug up to Bill, who looked like he was part of the sea. He had sandy brown hair, with a touch of gray, also a bushy mustache that covered his full lips that were always smiling, and showing his straight white teeth.

Gail, asked Bill, how long he had been captain of the Doc's boat. "I've been with the Doc, for ten years or more. I drive and do what ever he wants me to do. I guess you'd call me, his man Friday."

Being inquisitive, she asked, "How often do you bring people to the island?"

"Oh, quite often. The Doc, likes to have his friends stay at his place, and at the same time he knows that it's being kept up."

"But....what if I decide to leave the island, or get hurt. How would you know to come and get me?"

"There's a two way radio with instructions on how to use it. You just keep calling the Coast Guard and they will pick you up on there radio. In turn, they will relay your message to us." Sensing a note of fear in her voice, he quickly spoke up saying," Now don't you worry your pretty little head over it. You're going to have the time of your life."

"I hope so!" she answered, as she smiled back at him.

Gail's first glimpse of the island through binoculars, took her breath away. There was a long white sandy beach on one side with reefs and rock, that came out to form an inlet, where the water swelled up crashing against and over the rocks, only to race to the beach, then hurry back to the sea.

"OVER THERE!" came Bill's powerful voice, as he hollered to her and pointed. "There's the beach house!.....Up on the bluff....in the clearing!"

Yes she could see it now, and the stairs that led up to the side of the bluff. When she saw this, she got all excited inside." It's like an island you dream about! I love it!" Gail, yelled back to him.

Just then, large drops of rain started to fall, and before she knew it, Bill was telling her to go below, that it was just a little squall, and it would be over soon.

Little squall hell!... It seemed like a hurricane to her. She covered her ear's and closed her eye's, as the thunder and lightening rolled over them. Feeling a little ill, Gail laid down on the bunk and to her amazement, fell asleep. When she woke up, the storm had passed and the air had a clean, damp smell to it. Running her hands threw her hair she started up the steps to the deck, where Bill stood smiling at her," I see you made it!" he said, with a twinkle in his eye.

"Just barely, the water is so calm now, I don't understand the sea at all."

"It's like a woman," laughed Bill," all fire and fury one minute, and calm the next. We'll be coming up on the landing soon, and when we do, jump out and throw the rope around one of the pilings that are sticking up," commanded

7

Bill, in a powerful voice. When the time was right, Gail was quick to follow orders.

"Good Girl!...I'll make a sailor out of you yet!"

It took a while to get all the luggage and food up the stairs, and into the beach house. Once inside, Gail shrieked with joy. The house must have been built for a millionaire. When Gail asked, "who owned the house," Bill laughed, saying," A wealthy friend of mine."

"I'm sorry Bill, I didn't mean to put you on the spot like that. It's just that I didn't expect such a grand place."

"Well," said Bill, as he took a last look around, I had better be getting back. I'll see you in a couple of weeks. Then he smiled saying," Have fun!"

Before he could leave, Gail reached up and kissed his cheek, in turn, he gave her a big bear hug.

"See you soon!" called Gail, from the bluff above the cove.

Looking up, Bill's eyes blurred for the moment, as he wondered what could be wrong with this spunky little lady, that the Doc. had sent her to his hide-away to heal herself. "Heal yourself, little lady," he called into the wind, as he set course for home.

Once left alone, Gail closed and locked the door, then she laughed out loud at herself....Hell!.....who's going to come in? I'm the only one here. But, the door stayed bolted.

After she started a fire in the fire-place, to take the chill out, she put on her tapes and the room suddenly became alive. When she entered the first bedroom, it took her breath away, it was done all in pink, right there and then she decided not to look any further, as this would suit her just fine.

She put her clothes away, then decided to leave the rest until tomorrow.

When she stepped into the kitchen, Gail couldn't believe her eyes. Any woman would give her eye teeth for a kitchen like this. While putting away all the perishables, she was amazed at what was already in the refrigerator. Someone must have filled it knowing that she was coming. "How thoughtful of them," she thought. After eating a sandwich, she decided to take a shower and retire early, as she realized just how tired she was. Stepping out of the shower, she wondered who had decorated the bathroom, as it was rose colored and beautiful. The big plush towels, she had wrapped around herself, was soft and sweet smelling. With just the towel wrapped around her, she went into the front-room and made herself a night - cap.

As she poured the scotch into the glass, she said to herself, outloud." Oh what the hell....I may as well have one hell-of-a-drink, it might help me to sleep." Then she tipped the bottle up until the glass was more than half full. With that, she laughed, and poured just a splash of soda water into the scotch. As it went over her tongue and down her throat, her eyes teared for a moment, as she sighed, "Oh ya....that's good!" With the glass still in her hand, and the music filling the room, she had a great desire to dance.

Throwing her head back, she waltzed around the room, as if in a dream. "Whoops!...Can't let this towel fall," she said to herself, as her full breasts tried to rise above the towel, that was holding them so securely. Then turning, she checked the fire and turned off the tape, as she headed toward the bedroom.

All of a sudden, she felt as if someone was watching her, and the hair on the back of her neck stood up.....her heart started to pound, as she pulled the towel tighter around herself. She than forced herself to look out the window,..............and she gave a sigh of relief, as no one was there.

Once inside her bedroom, Gail slipped into a pair of blue silk pajamas, then quickly jumped into bed. She giggled to herself as she had visions of falling out of bed, as she had never slept between silk sheets before. She snuggled down and pulled the cover's up under her chin, and prayed that morning would come soon. She left the light on beside the bed, as if it were a protective guardian, watching over her sleeping form until dawn.

Drew Hatfield, had been staying at the Doc's beach house to recuperate from plastic surgery. He still needed a lot more surgery before the left side of his face would ever be normal again,..if ever. The doctor's had no guarantee on the finished product. Drew, had been a helicopter pilot, in the Marines, stationed in Vietnam. His face and arms had been burnt, as well as slashed by steel parts of the helicopter, when it had crashed. He had been in the Veterans Hospital in California, then sent to the burn center, for reconstruction on his face. There he met Dr. Philip Fresno. Not only was he his doctor, but they became good friends as well. Between the hospital and the burn center, a handful of doctor's pooled their money and set Drew up in a charter business, with the stipulation that when ever they wanted to go anywhere, or needed to send a patient from one hospital to another, that they would have top priority day or night.

The partnership was perfect! Drew, would talk to the clients on the phone, and his secretary would usher them on to the helicopter. This way, there was very little personal contact with the customers. He found, if he didn't turn his head, all they could see was the good side of his face. That way, he wouldn't have to see their eyes open wide with horror. He hated the way people looked embarrassed, when ever they looked at him, but the worst part was, the way they looked at him with pity, then turned their eye's away. Pity, was the last thing he wanted from anyone.

Drew, was walking along the beach on the other side of the island, when the wind picked up, bringing a cold chill with it. He walked a little faster, as the beach house came into view. When the smell of smoke hit his nostril's, he became enraged, for he didn't remember leaving the lights on, and he sure as hell hadn't made a fire in the fire-place!

Drew, sneaked up to the side of the house and carefully, and quietly went up the porch steps, then made his way to the front-room window, where the light was shinning through. Going closer, Drew, looked through the window......what he saw, made him step back, as not to be seen. His heart was pounding wildly. He didn't know if it was because someone else was there in the house.......or, because he was promised that no one else would ever be there,... but him! This alone made him furious.......or, was it what he saw?

For there, dancing around the living room, was a terrific looking lady, wrapped in a fluffy pink towel. Her honey colored hair flew out from her head, only to cling around her shoulders and beautiful face...He was spell bound by her beauty, and even as he felt himself hardening, he couldn't take his eye's off of her.........suddenly, the girl stopped dancing, and looked around at the window, with fright in her eye's. Drew, stepped back, as she came closer to the window. He leaned against the side of the house, as if he were part of it, until she finally shook her head and went back, only to pick up her glass and drain it's contents, then she put out the light's and disappeared.

11

Drew, let out his breath, and lit a cigarette.......only then, did he realize that his hand's were shaking. He decided to take a walk and to figure out what to do next, when just as he passed the other bedroom, a light came on..........and he knew that she was still frightened. Not wanting a hysterical women on his hands, he turned, and headed back to the beach. This wasn't first time he had slept on a beach, and it probably wouldn't be the last time either.

Who the hell the girl was puzzled him, and furthermore, what the hell was she doing there anyway? This wasn't the deal....he didn't want to see anyone, and he sure as hell didn't want anyone to see how hideous he was. He, had scared off enough people in the last few years, and he didn't want to add this girl to the list. He would find a way of telling her to leave....he was there first! And tomorrow, he would get rid of her for good!

CHAPTER TWO

The sound of the waves hitting against the rocks, awakened Gail from a sound sleep. She stretched, then laid back listening to the sound of the surf hitting the beach. Then in a flash, she jumped out of bed and started to dress. As she picked up her bra, she laughingly threw it back into the draw.....for there was no need to wear one here. Then, she picked up a T-shirt that had MAINE written on the front of it, and pulled it on over her head. Over her black lace panties, she pulled on her cut off dungarees. Either she had lost weight....or these weren't hers, as they were baggy in the rear. Maybe, Paul had been right....maybe she had lost weight. Stepping back, she looked into the full-length mirror. She looked terrible, she was pale and her hair was in tangles from tossing and turning all night. "Oh God!" she said to her reflection in the mirror. Picking up her comb, she began to pull it through her hair, once this was done, she felt and looked better. Then grabbing her sweater from the chair, she headed for the kitchen.

Gail, was singing, as she put the coffee pot on, then downed a glass of orange juice, while she put on her sneaker's. She poured herself a cup of coffee, then headed for the bluff, cup in hand. .

Soon she stood on the bluff over-looking the ocean. The morning air was nippy, pulling her sweater closer around herself, she wished that she had worn her jacket. Looking down, she noticed just how far down the stairs went, that tied into the dock. Gail, went and sat down in the dunes, where the tall grass sheltered her from the early morning wind. The tide was turning, and the water crashed angrily against the dock. After drinking her coffee, she laid back and watched the clouds roaming the sky, while the morning sun tried to break through.

Lying there, Gail realized for the first time, just how lonely she was. She had been on her own for a few years, and after getting out of the Navy, she liked having things just for herself. No more sharing everything and never having any privacy. All she wanted now, was for some one to put their arms around her, to hold her close..... for she was afraid for the first time, what tomorrow might bring.

Sitting up, she looked out over the sea and watched the constant roll of the waves. Some how it calmed her, and she felt as if a weight was being lifted off of her.

Meanwhile, on the other side of the island, a still form rolled over, and sat up. Drew, stretched as he glanced at the water's edge, then he thought of the girl, who had invaded his privacy. He, had to admit, that she had one hell of a body, and the way her hair fell across her shoulder's while she had danced, turned his insides into a knot. He, didn't want to get involved with anyone, especially now.......when he knew he had nothing to offer a woman. Turning abruptly, he swore as he headed back to the beach house where he would have it out with this girl, who ever she was.

Once there, he hesitated for a moment, then knocked on the door, being sure he was standing with his good side facing the screen door. When no one answered, he slowly opened the door and went inside. As he entered the kitchen, he could smell the coffee, and thought, "just what I need" He reached for a mug and filled it, then grabbed a handful of cookies from the shelf, and headed for the shower.

As he stepped into the shower, the warm water felt good on his stiff body, after sleeping on the beach all night. The warm soapy water felt good as it warmed his body while making little swirls and streams, that cascaded down over his broad muscular arms and shoulder's, that were marred by shinny scars, that had been there for awhile, then down to his narrow waist and strong powerful legs, that showed signs of working out. He was all of six feet tall and had thick brown hair, that went it's own way, His gentle brown eyes still showed signs of pain and disappointment in this life that had been dealt him. Stepping from the shower, he dried off, then wrapped the towel around himself and started to shave. This was a difficult job, as one side of his face was badly burnt, and the whiskers grew between the scars. His throat was another sensitive area. Every few days he would go back to the hospital, where the doctor or nurse, would shave him. For at this point, they could do a better job. While he tucked his shirt into his cut off jeans, that just covered the law, he glanced at the mirror.... his eye's going to a picture that was tucked into the side of the glass. He stared at the two young, good looking faces that smiled back at him. Then he swore, and covered his face with his hands, as a cold shiver went through him. The picture was of his buddy Frank, and himself. Frank had been the lucky one, as he had been thrown clear from the helicopter when it had crashed. A few broken bones, a few weeks in the hospital, then state side and home. They had kept in touch for awhile.....then the letters stopped coming. He gently touched the picture as he looked at himself in the mirror. He wasn't going to kid himself.... that smiling face was gone forever, and all his dreams with it. As he crushed the picture and threw it away, his eye's turned cold, as he turned to go out and find the young lady, that had dared to invade his privacy!

Feeling the sun beginning to break through, Gail, stood up and started to walk back to the beach house, to make breakfast for herself. If she wanted to sunbathe while the sun was at it's peak, she had better hurry

When Gail entered the house, she threw her sweater over the back of the nearest chair, then went to the refrigerator where she began to take out bacon and eggs. Soon the aroma of bacon frying, filled the room and floated out the open window, where the crackling noise it made, could be heard outside the screen door. There stood a man's tall form, watching her dropping eggs in to a skillet. For a moment, Drew wondered if he should eat first, or tell her to get out? The smell of bacon changed his mind. Turning his body so that his good side faced the screen door, he called, "Hello inside!"

Turning to face the door, with fear in her eye's, Gail screamed, "Oh God!....Who are you?" She felt her heart stop, when she realized that this stranger had been watching her. "Where did you come from?" she demanded. "How did you get here?......answer me buster!.....Or you'll wear this grease!" She held the frying pan in her hand, ready to throw it's contents at this intruder.

"Whoa....Wait a minute lady!.....I'm not here to harm you! You're trespassing...Not me, and I want to know, how you got here, and who the hell said you could eat my food?!" His voice exploded, making her shake down to her shoes.

Gail, couldn't see him clearly, because the sun was behind him. All she could make out was a dark outline of a man. One she hated on sight. Trespassing was she!....Well...who the hell did he think he was anyway?!

"Look....who ever you are, there must be some mistake. No one was to be here, but ME!.......He promised!!" she argued, with anger and determination in her voice.

"Who's he, and who are you?" "I'm Gail Hutton, and this place belongs to Doctor Philip Fresno, a friend of my brother-in-law's. This is his place, and I was told that I would be the only one here. Now, please leave the way you came." She was trying to keep control of her voice and talk calmly, with out letting fear creep into her voice. For, she had done this very thing, many times at the hospital.

"Look Lady, I was here first, and if you don't believe me, just go look in the bedroom................All my gear is there, and I've been here for day's!"

"All right," she, barely whispered, then she bellowed, "But, you better not move!" Gail, turned and ran to the back bedroom, where she pushed open the door.............There on the floor, were the clothes he had worn earlier, and a wet towel. She turned and ran into the bathroom, where the floor was still wet, where he had been standing. The smell of men's talcum was over whelming. 'Oh God!...Had he been in the house all this time? All at once she felt ill.....Something was terribly wrong!'

Suddenly, she heard the stranger yelling through the screen door......"When you can find time Lady, the eggs are being burnt to hell!"

. Running back to the kitchen, she could see smoke rising from the frying pan. "OH Damn It...Wait a minute!" she yelled back at the tall dark shadow. Lowering her voice, and feeling a little foolish after he had been telling her the truth, she asked," Who are you, and why are you here? While she talked, she dumped the blackened eggs into the sink, and started a fresh batch.

"My name is Drew Hatfield, and why I'm here is my own private business." Looking through the screen door, he could see that she was uneasy with him standing there, but he didn't want her to get a good look at him either, so..he quickly spoke up, saying, "Look, I don't know who you are, and I really don't care. All I want is to be left alone." Then he paused, adding, "We'll just have to work something out, so we can stay out of each others way, while we're here. So...let's call a truce for now, and you can pass my plate out the window, then I'll be gone for the day."

Gail, felt insulted and hurt, at the way this man was talking to her. 'Damn him.....she wanted her privacy too!' For a minute, she tried to remember if there was a lock on her bedroom door.

As if he knew what she was thinking, he spoke up in a loud voice," I hope you don't walk in your sleep, because I sleep in the raw, I also shower at night, and I expect to be able to get into the bathroom at a reasonable hour in the morning."

Being unable to hold her temper any longer, she snapped back at him, "Well of all the nerve!!... Look you jerk! Just keep out of my way, and keep your wet towels off the floor!" She stood there, her eyes blazing, as she squared off with him, her hands on her hips ready to argue at a minutes' notice. She could feel her face getting red as she realized just how personal the conversation had become.

Turning back to him, she started to put bacon and eggs on the two plates, along with a couple of buttered pieces of toast. Then poured two mugs of coffee. She then grabbed one of the plates and a mug and headed for the front door. Over her shoulder, she called back to him," I cooked breakfast, but you can go to hell and get it for yourself!"

When Drew saw Gail storm out of the kitchen, he slipped in and sat down to eat. While eating he thought, 'God....what a spitfire she is!' He remembered how her chest rose and fell as she had argued with him, and the way her dark eyes glared at him. Especially the way her voice shook, as she spoke. Even though she was afraid of him, as an intruder, she had a lot of spunk, and he could see that she was going to make the best of a bad situation. Then he remembered that his helicopter was on the other side of the island. Hell….. he could leave at any time! Or… better still, he could drop her off anywhere! Then speaking out loud to himself he mumbled, "No… I'll be damned if I'll leave. The island is big enough for the two of us!" Then he smiled as he thought,' She's a damn good cook, so why spoil things just yet.' After he had done the dishes, he stormed out of the kitchen, letting the screen door slam shut with a loud bang! Meanwhile Gail had found a quiet spot on the bluff, and now sat eating her breakfast while thinking of this arrogant stranger. She still had no idea what he looked like, as he had never faced her head-on. Oh well…what did she care what he looked like, just as long as he kept out of her way.

Later, she went back to the house and was surprised to find the dishes done, and no Drew in sight. Knowing that she was alone, she ran to her bedroom where she quickly changed into her new white two-piece bikini. She then grabbed her book and sunglasses, and throwing a towel over her shoulder, she headed for the beach. She was still fuming to think of sharing this place with anyone. Yesterday……it was like paradise….but today, she was all mixed up. 'If only he wasn't so damn rude and pigheaded!'

When she spotted the beach she let out a yell. It was beautiful! The sand was pure white and stretched as far as the eye could see. There were hardly any stones or shells to be had. Gail quickly spread out her towel, dropping both her book and glasses onto it. Then kicking off her sneakers, she ran toward the water. She stopped in her tracks as the ice cold water reached her ankles. "Oh!…..It's cold!…How can you be so cold and look so inviting?" as she called out to the sea. She then forced herself to run and dive in, only to come up and run out faster than she had entered. She dropped onto the towel, closing her eyes, as she sighed, "Boy….this is the life!"

Much later Gail could feel her back burning, and she rolled over. When out of the corner of her eye she spotted Drew walking along the cliff. His body was outlined by the sky, and as she watched him she couldn't help admiring his built. It was a well taken care of body, if she ever saw one! She knew he must have put oil on, as the sun glistened on his muscles, as he moved over the rocks. Unable to keep her eyes off him, she let her eyes travel up his strong legs and thighs, that let to a great set of buns. Closing her eyes she thought, 'Too bad he's such an ass!'

All kinds of questions ran through her mind. Why did she feel that he was hiding something from her?....What was he really doing on the island?....Was he a fugitive from the law?....And if so, what had he done? All she knew was that she had to find out….and soon!

The sun was stronger than Gail had realized and, she felt like a broiled lobster. Picking up her things, she headed for the beach house. If she hurried, she could take a shower before Drew came in. Just the thought of him being in the house gave her a scary feeling, knowing she knew nothing about this man.

When Gail removed her bathing suit, she was burnt more than she realized. When she stepped into the shower, she gave a sigh of relieve, as the warm water felt soothing on her skin and it was great to get the salt and sand out of her hair, and off of her body. While drying herself off she glanced at the mirror. There she saw a well rounded woman looking back at her, with light brown hair that hung past her shoulders, dark brown eyes and high cheek bones, a straight nose and full lips that smiled back at her. It was then, that she noticed that her skin was turning a deep red, where she had gotten sun-burned. Just her breasts were white except for the tips, where a soft brown surrounded her nipples. Her bikini bottom, being little more than a handkerchief, had left a white mark around her mound of soft light hair. Her shoulders hurt the most, while her face felt hot and tight, "Damn," she uttered, "I for got to pack my noxzema!,,,I'll never sleep tonight!" Then grabbing a soft tee-shirt and putting it on over her silk undies, she headed for the kitchen. Knowing that she had to pass through the front room, where Drew might be. 'Well, it's just to bad if he sees me dressed like this!' she thought to herself, 'This is my vacation......and if he doesn't like it, he doesn't have to look.'

It was against her nature to even think like this.....never mind parading around in front of a perfect stranger, with little more than a tee-shirt and a pair of silk pants, but she was hurting badly at that moment, and didn't give a damn!

Drew, was sitting in the front room, listening to the ball game, with his head resting on his chest as if he were asleep. Gail wanted to go closer, to get a good look at his face, but her thin tee-shirt stopped her. Instead, she hurried by, hoping he hadn't seen her.

When Gail entered the kitchen, there was a place all set up for her at the table. Drew, had left a note, telling her that she had made breakfast, so he had made supper, and her salad was in the refrigerator. Her steak was still in the frying pan, done to perfection. While she ate, she sipped on a glass of wine, that was cold and refreshing. By the time she had finished eating she felt a little guilty, as she thought about Drew. 'He could have eaten with her.............after all..... she didn't have a desease!'

21

Getting up from the table, she went into the front room to let him know that they could at least eat together. When she entered the living room she was suprised to see that he had left. "Good!" she said to herself, feeling a little hurt at the same time. She put on a tape and dropped into a chair, to finish reading her book, but her shoulders and back ached so badly that she wanted to cry. She kept squirming around in the chair until she could stand it no longer. Getting up, she decided to retire early, at least there she could remove all of her clothing......then maybe, the stinging pain would go away.

Earlier, when Drew had turned on the radio, he could hear the shower running and could picture Gail standing there with the water cascading down over her sensuous body. He remembered, how he had watched her from the cliff earlier, how he had looked her beautiful body over from head to toe....and how he had gotted a strange feeling in his loins. Even now.... as he watched her crossing the room, through half closed eyes, he noticed the swell of her breasts through her thin top, that left nothing to the imagination.

He told himself to get her out of his mind.........for he knew, he could never allow himself to ever have any feelings for any woman.....as long as he looked like he does now. He, suddenly realized that thinking about her and imagining her turning away, in horror, at his disfigurement, made his body break out in a sweat. Suddenly, he had to get out! He knew there would be times like this...when his body would betray him. He knew he had to keep his mind clear, and push all thoughts and feelings, that this spunky lady was creating in him, out of his life right now!! Before it was to late! He quickly snapped off the radio, then hurried out side, to take a walk along the beach. He would return much later, when he knew he wouldn't have to run into Gail again.

As he walked, the wind blew through his hair and fanned his body, cooling it down, while the steady rhythum of the tide, calmed the anger that raged within him. Tired and broken hearted, he walked untill he had walked a full circle, finding himself back at the beach house.

Drew, walked softly up the steps and along the porch, where he could see Gail through the window. He could tell she was in pain by the way she squirmed around in her chair. Then getting mad at himself, he thought, Why should I worry about her? Knowing that he had to put her out of his mind, he lit a cigarett, then just as quickly, put it out under his grinding foot.

Just as soon as Gail left the room, Drew slipped inside and went straight to the liquor cabnet, where he poured himself a stiff drink. Turning off the lights, he sat down in the darkened room, thinking about the girl in the next room, and wishing that things could have been different between them.

As he sat drinking, he could hear Gail tossing and turning, then he could have sworn he heard a sob. Getting up and going near her bedroom door, he could hear her softly crying. He couldn't stand to hear anyone in pain, he knew he had to do something to help her. He quickly went into the bathroom, where in the medicine cabnet he found a tube of salve for burns. Taking it from the shelf, he headed back to Gail's room.

Opening the door, he called softly to her, "Gail, please don't be frightened. I'm only here to help you." As Gail turned, and started to sit up, pulling the covers up to her chin, to hide her nudity, Drew quickly spoke up,

"NO!....Don't put on the light, I've got something to put on your sunburn."

"Thanks Drew but I'll be alright," she answered, in a shaky voice, while trying to wipe her tears away, "Please.......just go away!"

As he stept closer to the bed, she could feel his presence and she panicked for the moment, as she was nude under the sheet. Her heart was beating wildly. and she felt a strange warm feeling inside her, for his voice was soft and full of compassion..................

"Please, I only want to put some salve on your sunburn."

Before, she could answer or pull away, he had tenderly pulled the sheet down to her heaving breasts. Then he gently smoothed the cool salve over her arms and shoulders, then ever so carefully on her face, even though she flinched at his soft touch The room was so dark, that hard as she tried to see his face, it was impossible, as he kept it turned away from her.

He told her to roll over, then he pulled the sheet further down to where her bikini bottom had left it's mark. He stopped when he could see the whitness of her beautiful rounded bottom. Then he slowly smothed the salve over her shoulders, and down to the small of her back,

"Hummm........that feels so good!" she sighed, as he slowly pulled up the sheet to just below her bottom. When he gently smoothed the salve over her calfs and thighs, he could feel the heat from her body, and he hoped that she hadn't gotten sun stroke as well. If she hadn't been in so much agony, he would have lingered over her body a lot longer, for the touch of her skin stired him emotionally as never before.

Straightening up, he said, in a tight strange voice, "I hope you'll be able to sleep now. If you need me, for anything, call and I'll hear you."

"Thanks Drew, I feel better already," she whispered, as she hugged her pillow closer in her arms. She smiled, as she heard him close the door softly, knowing he wasn't the tough guy he pretended to be.

After Drew showered, he wrapped a towel around himself, then headed for his bedroom, where he threw himself across the bed and reached for a cigarett, on the night-stand. Lighting it, he took a long slow drag, then let out the smoke slowly, thinking,....all he had wanted to do was to help this lady out..... but instead, the feel of her skin under his touch stirred memories, memories he thought he had pushed aside for ever. He had promised himself, along time ago that he would never let himself love again... but Oh God... how her skin felt so soft under his hands.....how he had wanted to take her into his arms and kiss all her pain away. He could still see her body in the moonlight, that had filtered in through the window,giving her skin a soft glow, that drove him crazy for something that was beyond his reach! With a groan, he rolled over, putting out his cigarett, as a silent tear slid down his face. For she....like all women, were out of his reach forever.

When Gail, realized that Drew was in her bedroom, she had panicked.....but now...all she could think of was how his hands had felt on her body. Of how she had gotten a wierd sensation down low, one that she had never experenced before. She had wanted desperately to roll over, to hold him close and run her hands over his body, as he had done to her. 'God,' she thought, 'how can I feel this way when I don't even know him and I 've never seen his face?' Still… she felt a need for this man,…..A need that gave her no peace.

Later, as she layed awake thinking, her thoughts went to the burn center and to her patients. She remembered how their pain was so unbearable at times and how she would try to help them, as Drew, had done for her tonight. She remembered how she would hold the little ones and kiss their scared faces, that were so badly disfigured, that they really didn't care if they lived or died. She never saw them as ugly, only as someone who was beautiful on the inside, and in need of love. This she could give to them. Tears ran unchecked down her face, as she tried not to think of the children, that were waiting for her return.

Gail, woke the next morning to the sun shinning in on her and a persistant knock on the door. Drew's voice came drifting through the door, telling her that her breakfast was on a tray, and that he would leave it by the door. Then there was silence.

"I'm coming!" she called back, as she jumped out of bed wrapping the sheet around herself as she opened the door, only to find the hallway empty, and her tray where Drew had left it. Looking toward the living room, she called out to Drew, but she knew the house was empty once again. As she ate, her thoughts went back to the man that had fixed her breakfast, and she wondered for the first time, what terrible thing had he done, to always be hiding from her……….as if she would reconize him. Maybe, if she could get him to talk to her, he would open up….then maybe things would be better between them.

Gail, stayed around the house all day as she didn't want to get burnt, anymore than she already was. It was past lunch time and she hadn't seen Drew all morning. She wondered what he did with his time, as she had noticed that he always went off in the same direction. He was so mysterious, that her womens intuition took over. Tomorrow I'll track him down! Hell, this is worse than being alone.....to know that he's here but never to see him, and when I do, all we do is argue. Funny though.....at night, when it's dark, and I can't see his face, he's so different. Then he's soft spoken, gentle and considerate. Hadn't he shown her that last night??

Thinking of last night, she could still feel the touch of his hands, like a caress, as they had slowly moved over her body, awakening desires that she had never known before. All she knew was that she wanted and needed more of this man's touch. Gail smiled to herself, as she had never felt this way about any man that she had ever dated. Let alone a perfect stranger. Well.... I'm not going to think about him any longer. Getting up she headed for the porch and the lounge, that beckoned to her. Throwing herself down on it, she realized that she couldn't keep her mind off of him, even for a minute While she peeled an orange for herself, she thought, 'This is my vacation and I'm going to enjoy it! Anyway.....Drew had never asked her where she lived or what she did for a living. Mabe, he doesn't really care who I am.' Gail felt both hurt and angry at this. Finishing her orange, she tried to read her book, but found she couldn't concentrate on it. Dropping the book to the floor, she closes her eyes, and let the gentle breeze of the water lull her to sleep.

Drew got up early that morning and not wanting to awaken Gail,he decided to take a swim instead of a shower, as he had listened to her tossing and turning most of the night. Pulling on his bathing trunks and a pair of worn out sneakers, he threw a muscle shirt over his arm and headed for the kitchen. There he made breakfast for the two of them. When he had finished his, he put Gail's on a tray and took it to her room. Putting it down outside the door, he knocked and told her it was there. When he heard the bed creek, he knew she was up and heading for the door. Hearing this, he turned and hurried out of the house. He heard her calling to him but instead of answering her, he began to run. He didn't stop running until he was within sight of the helicopter, then he sat down to catch his breath.

"Damn it!!....Why don't I just get in the damn thing and leave!"

He, argued with himself. No he knew he couldn't leave just yet. What if she got sick from the sunburn that she had gotten......who would be there to help her? He knew in his heart that this was just an excuse to stay,..... then why did he care what might happen to her? She meant nothing to him.....or did she? After he had cooled down, he walked to the waters' edge and watched the angry sea crashing against the rocks. He could tell the under-toe would be bad but he had nothing to loose, so why not go for it! When he plunged into the water, it was frigid, and he was chilled to the bone. He felt a tremor ripple through his body, as it relaxed, leaving him calm and in control of his feeling once more. As he walked toward the helicopter, he pushed back his hair and decided to do some work on it.

His ignitor plug was fouled, there for he had to do some preventive maintenance, before he would be able to leave the island.

Leaning into the chopper, he pulled out his ditty bag and went to work.

Drew, didn't realize how late it had gotten, until a cold chill passed over him and he knew that the tide was beginning to change. He was dirty, sweaty and tired, but he felt better than he had in a long time. He had been so depressed lately, and hadn't cared what happened to him....that was one of the reasons that the doctor's had decided to put a stop to all of his surgery. Doctor Phil, as he called him, told him to take a few weeks off, and to try and snap out of his depression, for his attitude was very important at this time. Well, he had taken his advice and maybe it was working, for all of a sudden he felt alive again. After cleaning off his tools, and putting them away, he locked up the chopper and headed for the beach house.

The sun had gone down leaving a chill in the air. When Drew was a short distance from the house, he smelt smoke coming from the chimney and realized that Gail must have lit a fire in the fire place. Seeing a light on in the kitchen, Drew, figured Gail would be cooking supper,so to avoid her, he went around to the front door, where he quietly slipped in.

Drew went directly to the bathroom where he stripped away his clothes and stepped into the shower. As he stood there, he wondered what it would be like to have Gail there with him. He could visualize her with soap suds swirling down over her full breasts, which he knew were milk white, then down over her flat stomache and further down to her beautiful legs,...........legs that he had felt, only the night before. Feeling himself hardening, he turned on the cold water full blast, and that brought him back to reality. A few minutes later as he stood there shaving, a knock came to the door. "Drew, can you hear me? I've got supper made, so.. why don't we eat together for a change?" Getting no answer she hesitated before she said "I promise not to argue with you. What do you say? Let's call a truce!"

Drew closed his eyes, as he leaned against the sink…God!..She can't see me like this! He knew the lights would be on, so the only way he could make her eat alone and leave the kitchen,was to be rude to her again. Holding on to the sink, he drew in his breath, before he could answer her.

"Look Lady!" he bellowed. Then in a real sarcastic tone of voice, he said, "I didn't ask you to cook for me, and I told you before, that I wanted my privacy!………So for Christ sakes….LEAVE ME ALONE!"

He heard a muffled sound of suprise come from her, then in a chocked voice, she yelled back. "Mr. Hatfield, go straight to hell!..…..and I hope you choke on supper….and… and you had better enjoy it, because it's the last thing I'm ever going to cook for you!!……You'r a tempermental bastard,…..and I don't care what kind of trouble you're in,and I really don't care who you are or what you look like!"

Gail, was so shocked at what he had said to her, that her eyes filled with tears and her throat tightened up as she raged on," And my name is Gail Hutton,…….Not LADY!" Then with a sob, she cried, "Go stay in your little world of darkness….because I'm through trying to be nice to you!"

Drew, could hear her sob as she tried to speak…….but when he heard her turn and run to her room, banging the door behind her, he wanted to die. God…what had this woman ever done to him, except try to be friendly. He knew he was being drawn to this woman that had so much fire in her. She could cut a man down to size,and yet,…..he remembered how the very touch of her skin had turned hin to jello. He stood there, clinging to the edge of the sink, when what he really wanted to do was to run after her and fold her in his arms, while begging her forgiveness, as he kissed away her tears. He tried to tell himself that it was better to hurt her now, than have her find out the truth about him later, and end up pitying him. No!.....If he couldn't have this woman, than he wanted no part of her.

Drew, splashed cold water on his face then looked at himself in the mirror. His face was scarlet from shaving, and as he looked at himself, He spoke aloud, in a strained voice, "Every time I start to forget who I am, I'll just take a look in the mirror to remind me!"

When Gail's sobs subsided, she couldn't understand Drew's actions. He was like hot and cold water. Why did he have to be so nice to her one minute, and then so damn arrogant the next? Wiping her eyes and blowing her nose, she lifted her chin and walked out of the bedroom as a woman in total control of herself. She wasn't going to let a good meal go to waste. She sat down and tried to eat a cold supper. She was still so furious inside, that she would have eaten it, even if it had been a frozen dinner! After she had eaten and cleaned her dishes, she left the remaining food right where it was. He could heat his own supper if he wanted any of it.

Having had the chills all day, Gail made a fire in the fire-place, then made herself a tall scotch and soda and went and sat in front of the fire. She had been gazing into the fire when suddenly she felt his presence behind her. With out turning around, she asked sarcastically, "What do you want now?"

"Nothing Gail, I just wanted to apologize for being a damn fool. I don't know why....but you rub me the wrong way."

"Well....I'd hate to think of how you'd act if I rubbed you the right way!" she snapped back at him, adding," You don't have to worry Drew, I won't bother you or get in you way again.....I'll stay out of your sight, and just pretend that you're not even here." Her voice was full of emotion and she was very near tears again.

Sensing this, he knew that he had to break all ties now....before she got hurt again. Speaking up quickly, he answered, "Great! Then we have nothing to worry about! You just take care of your needs and I'll take care of mine." His voice was husky and strained, but there was a sadness in it, and this puzzled her.

"I have things to do in my life," he added "and I haven't any room in it for any woman..... I'll admit, you're not bad looking,..... but your just not for me!" Then without another word, he turned and abruptly walked out into the night.....leaving her there sputtering to herself, with her eyes blazing!

"Well of all the nerve! Who does he think he is? No room for women! Who the hell would want him anyway,' she thought, as she got up and made herself another drink. Then she raised her glass toward the door, that he had just closed behind him, saying out loud, "Here's to you and your secrets, but starting tomorrow I'll be watching you..... and if your watching me too........Look OUT! Because I'll make you want me, then I'll break your heart, like you just broke mine." She didn't realize that she was crying, until a tear fell into her drink

Had she said," He broke her heart?" He was probably a thief, or worse, but in her heart she knew there was something between them ....and she had to find out if he felt the same as she.....or did he really want her out of his life forever? For the more he tried to push her away, the stronger her feelings for him grew. Damn it! Why was her body betraying her now? It was like he had taken over her emotions........turning them on and off at will.

During the night, Drew tossed and turned in his bed, knowing that he had hurt Gail's feelings. Now all he wanted to do was to take her in his arms and hold her and never let her go, to tell her that he was falling in love with her. He ached all over as he pictured her in his arms, knowing that she could never be anything but a fantasy of his imagination.

With a groan, he rolled over burying himself deeper into the pillow, as if to blot out all his desires. "God!..How I need and want her beside me. Now...Tonight," he whispered into his pillow. It took a long while before sleep finally took over....giving him peace at last.

The next few days were hard on both of them, Gail, tried to put Drew out of her mind, but found herself constantly watching for a glimpse of him. She loved the way his muscles on his arms glistened with sweat, as he swept away the sand from the porch steps, or when he was stacking wood against the shed out back. She found herself falling in love, and not being able to do anything about it. Drew still kept his distance during the day,...but at night, when it was dark, he would talk to her but only if she started the conversation. For some strange reason, she felt drawn to this man, as if he were a magnet. She knew he felt the heat of her desire, when ever they were in the same room, but... he had a secret that was keeping them apart, and this secret, was what she had to find out.....then....just maybe, they could become friends......or more....

The next morning, when Gail heard the door swing shut, she jumped out of bed, for today she was going to follow Drew, to where ever it was that he went every day. She

33

quickly put on her halter top, and a pair of cut off jeans, with nothing under them, No one was around, so why not enjoy being free of her undies. 'Maybe I should have burnt my bras when everyone else was burning theres.' Still laughing to herself, she run out of the house in pursuit of Drew.

Gail followed close by then she spotted him. As she climbed down into a clearing, there to her amazement she saw a red and white helicopter! Damn him!!....He could have left anytime he wanted! Now what was he doing? She watched from above as he took out tools and started to work on the engine. 'Now I get it,' she thought to herself, 'he had engine trouble and landed here, and seeing that no one was living at the beach house, he broke in and just took over!' All sorts of crazy thoughts went through her mind. Was he a drug dealer?.......Was he wanted by the F.B.I.?? Was that the reason why he didn't want her to see him up close?....Was he afraid that she would recognize him? Suddenly, her mind was torn between love and fear for this stranger....Then speaking in a whisper, she spoke to the back of this mystery man, "Tomorrow I'll bring my binoculars,........then Mr.Hatfield I,ll get a good look at you, who ever you are!" Gail, stayed hidden and watched Drew working, until he took time out for a swim. He was a powerful swimmer and her heart pounded faster with each stroke he took. When he finally came out of the water, he stretched out on the warm sand, his body glistening in the sun. Gail's eyes roamed over his shoulders, then slowly down to where his bathing suit was now clinging to his anatomy, clearly showing his manhood. She pictured herself lying on top of him, running her hands through his hair, then down over his masculine smooth body. She suddenly got a tight funny sensation between her legs, and that brought her back to reality. 'What had she been thinking?' Her face felt flushed, and she knew it wasn't from the sun. Slowly, she turned and walked away.

Later that afternoon, as Gail walked along the beach, she suddenly realized that she was being watched from the sand dunes above.

Well, if Drew was watching her, she would give him an eye full, just to shake him up, and see what would happen. She smiled to herself, as she started to undo her halter top. She walked a few feet with the knot undone between her breasts, letting herself be exposed to him, as she continued walking. Then she took it completely off, and walked a few yards more to where she knew he would be watching her. Then she stopped, letting the halter fall to the sand,as she undid the zipper on her shorts, letting them drop to her ancles. Stepping out of her geans, she quickly turned to face the ocean, so he couldn't see her blush, with embarrassment,as she had never done anything like this before in her life! She couldn't understand what was making her act this way! She walked slowly toward the ocean, then suddenly ran and dove in......only to come up with a shriek, for the water was ice cold! She stayed in and found that she was enjoying herself. After diving into the waves and riding them in Gail decided to get out of the water. Feeling a little foolish at what she had done, she looked up toward the sand dunes and had the feeling that she was alone once more.

Drew watched Gail as she walked out of the water, her hair was clinging to her back and shoulders, and he knew he would never see such a lovely sight ever again. Her body moved in perfect motion as she walked, her beautiful full breast rose and fell with each step she took. He loved the way the sun glistened on her wet skin that was tanning up nicely, except for where her bathing suit went. He suddenly had a desire to posses this lovely creature, and to kiss and lick every little drop of water from her beautiful body. He became aware of his passionate desire, as he felt himself hardening, against his trunks, that was begging for release. With a muffled groan, he burried his head in his arms, and laid very still until he knew she had left the beach.

Later that night, Drew sat alone in the front room, in the dark. He held a drink in one hand, while staring at the floor deep in his own thoughts.

Not being able to sleep,Gail heard Drew,as he walked past her bedroom door. Aparently, he couldn't sleep either, so she got up and put on a short, white satin, wrap-a-round over her white lace underpants,then header for the front room.

What a strange man he was....for there he was drinking all by himself in the dark. Well, if this is how he wanted it,...that was all right with her. She walked slowly into the darkened room, pretending that she hadn't seen him sitting there. Going over to the bar, she fumbled around in the dark, fixing herself a drink. Then as she turned, she pretended to see him sitting there.

"Oh! I didn't know you were in here," she lied, in a soft sexy voice."Do you mind if I sit here in the dark with you?" Then before he could answer her, she sat down opposite him on the couch, saying," I promise not to talk, unless I'm spoken to."

"No...I don't mind, if you don't mind sitting in the dark. I like it better this way." He spoke in a gentle voice and she was glad she was there. She finally broke the silence with idle chatter. Gail, asked him if he had gone swimming. Then waited,to see if he would lie to her.

As he looked through the darkness, he could make out her out line, against the moon- light, that filtered in through the window behind her.

"Ya....I was able to get in a few laps today. Did you get to take a swim?" His eyes sparkled and a slow smile spread across his lips, as he remembered how she had looked coming out of the water. He could still see her naked body all pink and moist, and his heart beat faster, arousing him as never before. He took a long drink, from his glass as he studied her every move.

"Yes, I went in for a swim....in fact, I did something today that I've never done before. I went skinny dipping," she laughed, blushing at the same time, as she continued talking. "I never felt so good in my life." Then looking directly at him, she asked, "Why don't you come with me some night, and try it for yourself? It would be dark, the way you like it. I've always wanted to swim at night,.....but I'm afraid to swim alone."

"He smiled and laughed out load, for the first time, saying, "We'll see.....maybe." Gail, laughed back with delight, "Thanks Drew, we'll have fun,...I know it!"

Fun, yes....If he could keep himself in control. After all, in the dark, he was vulnerable. Anything could happen! There it was again, that terrible urge to take her in his arms, to kiss her smiling lips, until he had his fill. Just then, Gail stood up saying," You have a wonderful laugh, you know. You should exercise it more often." With that, she stood up stating, "Good night," and walked slowly to her room.....Once there, she crawled into bed, wishing that Drew had followed her. She fell asleep day-dreaming of him making love to her.

Drew finished his drink, and as he put his glass down he thought of Gail, how she had looked sitting there in that soft

37

white robe, which moved ever so gently, as she breathed, and moved about on the couch. He had wanted to reach out and infold her in his arms, to touch and feel the weight of her breasts in his hands. When he closed his eyes he could almost feel the softness of her beautiful body, that was surounded by smooth,white satin. His blood ran hot in his veins as he felt himself getting sexually aroused, just thinking of her.

He, knew he was falling for her, and that he would have to keep himself in control, so no one would get hurt........no one but himself. This thing about skinny dipping.........Well, that was another matter. After all,......no matter what he looked like, he was still very much a man,....and he wanted and needed her desperately. He,was in no hurry to go to bed, for he knew.........there would be little sleep for him tonight!

Gail,watched Drew from her bedroom window as he left the house and walked along the same path as yesterday. Moving from the window, she hastily went through her suit cases until she found her binoculars. Slinging the strap over her shoulder, she headed for the kitchen. As she gulped down her coffee, she began to get excited, for today, she would get to see just what Mr. Right looked like!

Gail was about to leave, when she heard a buzzing sound coming from the counter. Turning, she saw a light flashing on the two-way radio. She quickly picked up the receiver, while reading the directions on how to use it. Then all of a sudden, Bill's voice came in, load and clear

"Gail, this is Bill. How are you doing? Over!"

"Fine Bill, I love it here. Over!"

"Gail, have you seen a man and his helicopter on the island? Over!"

Suddenly Gail felt a cold chill pass through her. Were the police looking for him? She knew, she had to protect him, so she said," no! ....Why? Over."

"Don't be alarmed. Someone back here, want's him pretty badly. If you see him, call me Over."

"Yes Bill, I will, Bye for now. Over."

As she slowly hung up the receiver, she knew, she had lied for Drew. She, just had to find out what kind of trouble he was in. She had to warn him! Oh why, did this have to happen now, when there was only one more week left on the island. Not now!....When she realized that she loved him passionately, no matter what he had done!

Walking softly, Gail crept to the same spot as the day before. There, she took out her binoculars and raised them to her eyes. As she looked the chopper over carefully, a pair of masculine legs came into view, bringing a smile to her face. Slowly, she raised them up to his perfectly shaped bottom, that was covered by a tight,black, skimpy bathing suit, as he stood with his back to her, the persperation on his arms and shoulders glistened in the sunlight,as he labored over the engine. All she wanted to do at this moment, was to trail her fingertips over his shoulders and down his back.

She could almost feel the smooth skin under her palms. She found herself swallowing hard and holding her breath, as she continued to watch his muscle's ripple as he worked.

"Turn around," she kept repeating, to herself. "Boy...are you handsome "! She whispered, as he turned his good side toward her. "Now turn all the way around, so I can see all of you!" Just then, he bent down to pick up a tool, and when he straightened up, he looked directly at her, as if by comand.

"OH GOD, NO!! "She cried, as she looked at his disfigured face. Her eyes filled with tears, as she put the binoculars down, "Oh Drew, is this what you've been hiding from me?" she cried, for this man she loved, and for all the pain and agony, that she knew went hand in hand, with this kind of disfigurement. She cried softly to herself, 'don't you know I don't care…I see this every day of my life………No wonder you didn't want me to see you.' Suddenly, all her fears were gone. He, wasn't a crook! Deep down she had known it, but now,what was she to do? She knew if she told him of her discovery, he would panic and leave the island,…..unless he loved her too,….then maybe, she could convince him of their need for each other. Also that love was based on more than just good looks and a few scars. While she walked back to the beach house, all she could think of was how and what she could do to convience him of this.

Gail spent the better half of the after-noon doing laundry. The wind was so warm and strong that the sheets dried, almost as fast as she hung them. As she touched the sheets fron his bed, she burried her face in them, wishing that she could share them with him.

Later that night, as she layed in bed, tossing and turning, she suddenly could no longer stand not being near him. She loved him so desperately, that she couldn't bear the thought of being anywhere but in his arms. Gail knew, she had to be the first one to make a move or they would be lost forever. Gathering up all her courage, she slipped out of bed and headed for Drew's room.

When she entered his room, he stired, asking, "Who's there? "It's only me." she whispered, in a nervice tone of voice. Then going closer to his bed, her heart began to beat harder and faster,while her mouth felt dry. What if he told her to leave? Her heart stopped beating for a moment. Then his husky voice came through the darkness.

"Gail,.....you shouldn't be here like this."

Going closer to him, she sat on the edge of the bed near enough so she could feel the heat from his body, as she whispered, in a soft loving tone, 'Oh Drew, I need you so," then leaning over she kissed him at the same time. He quickly turned his head, so her kiss would land on his good side, as his hands went to her arms, as if to ward them off.

"Gail, please," he pleaded, in a strained voice," Don't do this. You'll only be hurt! I have nothing to offer you.....Please go!.... Before it's to late!"

"It was too late, the minute I stepped into this room," she whispered, as she laid her palms on his bare chest, then slowly let them encircle his body. All the while, she placed kisses in the hallow of his throat, and on up to his face. He kept his head turned, and she didn't force him to look at her, instead, she murmured, "Make love to me .....now....I need you so."

A groan, that could not be held back, escaped from his throat, as he scooped her into his arms, holding her locked within his powerful embrace into her hair, he whispered," God forgive me, for you may hate me tomorrow, but for tonight you're mine!"

He kissed her hair, her eyes, then her lips that trembled beneath his own, and fireworks exploded in his head. He kissed her neck, while he pulled her down onto the bed beside him. In between kisses, he gently began to remove her nightgown and as his hand passed over her breasts, they became hard and firm to his touch. Feeling a need for him to touch her as never before, she reached up and burried her fingers into his hair as she pulled his head down to her breast. When she felt his tongue gently tease her nipples, she drew his head in closer to her breasts, then he gently bit them, one at a time, always going back to her lips for more.

41

This time when he kissed her, he ran his tongue over her lips.. and with a sigh she parted them for him to enter and to explore. He moaned and deepened the kiss,as their tongues teased, and caressed each other,.......untill Gail broke away whispering into his shoulder, "Oh Drew, I knew it would be like this.........I love you so."

Upon hearing this, he trailed his hands down over her full breasts, then down around to feel her smooth bottom, then futher down her thigh where he slid his hand up the inside of her thigh, to touch and fondle her where she was warm and moist to the touch.

Gail's hands had been all over his back, and now he could feel her reaching down to take hold of his manhood. "Oh God...It feels so good, "he passionately whispered, between deep gasps of air, "I've dreamed of you doing this so often." As a groan came from her throat, he rolled her over, and raised himself above her. As he entered her, she gave a little gasp, which told him everything, when he raised up and thrust again, deeper and harder, as if he couldn't get enough of her.

Gail reached her arms around him until she held him by his bottom, pulling him in closer to take all of him, never wanting to let him go. She wrapped her legs around him, imprisoning him inside her. With their arms locked around each other, they moved in rhythm as one, whispering little words of passion, hightening their desire for each other. In their mad passion to please one another, Drew didn't realize it at first, that she had kissed and touched his face and nothing terrible had happened. As he felt their passion mounting, he thrust harder, as she called out his name, as they climaxed together. They held each other untill the trembling stopped, for he couldn't bear to be apart from her......not just yet.

He rolled over bringing her with him, as if to make it last a little longer. He kissed her beautiful face, as she lifted herself up onto her side to look at him. "I love you Drew. Whatever is troubling you, I can handle it. Please, let me help you?" Before he could answer, she leaned down and gave him a kiss, that he would never forget. She parted her lips and drew his in gently, playing with his tongue, then nibbling at his lip. She kissed his eyes, his nose and both sides of his face, very gently, while crooning that she loved him.

All of a sudden, Drew realized what she had been doing, and a lump came to his throat. For a while he had forgotten who.....and what he was....as tears sprang to his eyes, then slid slowly down his face, he pushed her away and sprang to his feet.

"Drew! ...What's the matter? ..... Tell me, please darling...don't shut me out!" She realized, she was crying too, as she went to him where he stood near the window trying to control himself. She stood behind him, their naked bodies touching as she rested her head in the middle of his back and hugged him to her. It broke her heart to feel the agony that he was going through. "Please darling," she begged, through tears, "let me help you."

"No Gail, please.......just leave me alone! I never meant for this to happen. It's not you darling.....It's me! I never should have taken advantage of you,....or anyone else," he stated, as he gently but firmly pushed her arms away from him, then went to the bed, where his robe was waiting. "I love you Gail," he confessed, "but there's no room in my life for you ....or any other woman."

"No! Don't say that, I don't believe you! How can you make love to me as you just did, and then tell me it's over? I thought you loved me!" then she broke down, her sobs

43

racked her body, for she knew deep down in her heart, that no matter what he had said now,he didn't mean it. He just didn't want to straddle her with a disfigured lover. "Oh Drew," she pleaded, "can't you feel how much you mean to me?"

"Please Gail,It's because I love you so much that I have to let you go." His heart was breaking and he yearned to turn around and take her in his arms and never let her go, but instead.....he put on his robe and left the room.

When the door closed behind Drew, she knew that in loving him....she might just have lost him. No!...I can't loose him now! She had fought for the kids on her ward, when they wanted to throw in the towel. Well....he was worth the fighting for,....and this was only round one! She would never give up on him, or their love for each other. Never!...Never!

The next day, Gail watched as Drew worked on the helicopter. She realized that he was finished, when he quit early. Now he was free to leave the island, any time he wanted.

Gail wanted to run down and throw her arms around him and tell·him that she didn't care what he looked like, just as long as he loved her, but she knew it would have to come from him. She had only four days left and she was dying inside, because she needed him in her life. With a heavy heart, she went back to the beach house and gathered up her casting rod and headed for the inlet side of the island.

She had come here to fish and maybe by doing this she could keep her mind off Drew for a little while. She had been casting and reeling in for a couple of hours, when suddenly she couldn't stand the silence any longer. Gathering up her fishing gear, she headed slowly back to the beach house. All the way back her thoughts of Drew leaving, were driving her mad. She had to do something, and fast!....Before he decided to leave!

There she was, twenty-five with a good job that was driving her slowly into a depression, and now.... here on this island, she had to meet and fall in love with a man that could not except her for what seemed to her a crazy vain reason of his own. She remembered the call from Bill, and decided that since Drew was not a gangster, as she had thought, he had better get in touch with who ever it was that was looking for him.

Gail had just finished showering, when she heard Drew come in. She opened the bathroom door, and called out, "Drew, call Bill, he has a message for you!"

"Thanks Gail. I'll give him a ring right now."

Gail could hear Drew talking, but couldn't hear what was being said. She had a feeling in the pit of her stomach, that he would be leaving soon, and she would never see him again.

Gail, was busy in the kitchen, when she decided to take one more chance, and break down his resistance. She went to his bedroom door, and knocked softly, saying, "Drew, I've packed a cookout to have on the beach. Why not put on your suit, and I'll meet you there after dark?"

Getting no answer, she tried again, "Drew...Did you hear me?"

"YEA....maybe later," answered Drew, in a strained tone of voice.

Later, as she sat on the beach, waiting for Drew, she made a fire. On a blanket, she had put potato salad, and sliced tomatoes, and all the fixing for a cook-out. All that was left to do, were the hot dogs. She had taken the last four

45

bottles of cold beer, and they were getting warm. Where was he? Maybe, he wouldn't come after all. Just as she started to pick up the plates, she heard him walking toward her. "I'm so glad you came when you did. I was about to give up."

"Well, now that I'm here, let's eat, drink, and be merry, for tomorrow we die!" He tried to laugh, as if it were a joke, but Gail looked away, as she sensed that this would be their last night together. 'Damn him! didn't he know she was dying a little inside?'

When they were through eating, Drew leaned back on his elbow, saying, "that was great. I didn't realize I was that hungry." As he talked, he studied her face, a face that he would never forget.

"Me neither, by the way....did you get in touch with your friend?"

"Yea....I took care of everything." He, wasn't going to volunteer any information to her, so she let the subject drop.

Later, as they sat in silence, side by side, Gail turned and looked at Drew, then very casually said, "I'm going skinny dipping, want to come?" Then before she could change her mind, she quickly started to undress. As she turned, the moonlight played across her body, and he held his breath at her beauty.

Had he heard right?....Had she said, "skinny dipping?" He swallowed hard, as she held out her hand to him, saying, "come on, don't be chicken!"

"Who's chicken!" he laughed back, as he removed his trunks in one quick sweep, then ran after her into the surf.

They were horsing around in the surf, when she landed in his arms. The minute her body came in contact with his, he knew he couldn't resist her. With a groan, he threw abandonment to the wind, and gathered her close in his arms, while the waves broke over them. Gail stood on her toes, as each wave broke over them, again and again, trying to pry the two lovers apart. Before this could happen, Drew lifted Gail up to his height, and she wrapped her legs around his waist, and hung on. He kissed her salty lips, as his need for her grew, feeling himself hardening, he deepened his kisses, and drank in the taste of her hungry mouth.

"Please Drew," she called over the sound of the waves, "I'm drowning! Can't we go to the blanket?"

Never saying a word, he picked her up in his arms and carried her to the waiting blanket. There he continued to break down all her reserves. He kissed and caressed her until she was like a wild thing under him. She kissed him passionately, kiss for kiss, between sobs, and little moans of pleasure. He maneuvered her, until she was straddling him, leaving her in control. As they rocked in motion, he kissed her breasts and teased her nipples between his teeth, until she moaned and called out his name, as her passion mounted. Hearing this, he held her tightly in his embrace, and rolled over, bringing her with him, his lips never leaving her, as he took control once again. They strained together, trying to hold on to each other more intimately than ever before. As he thrust harder and deeper, he felt her body trembling beneath him, "Drew, Oh Drew," she sobbed, into his shoulder. He thrust slower and harder, as he felt himself getting ready to explode within her. "Ahhhh....ohh Gail..." he whispered into her hair, as their bodies ceased to tremble. Hearing her softly crying, he fell to kissing her with a hunger, that would have to hold him for the rest of his life.

He knew he loved this woman that lay in his arms, and he knew that leaving her would be the hardest thing he had ever done...but she had to be free, to find some other man.

One who would love her, and give her a family. She was too beautiful and loving to ever be an old maid. But God!....How was he ever going to let her go? With a surging pain in his heart, he gave a pitiful groan, as he gathered her closer in his arms once more. He didn't know what was in store for him,....and he couldn't put her through the test. He just kept holding her close to his heart, while kissing her, as if to draw strength from her body.

Gail knew by the pressure of his arms, that he was fighting a battle within himself. She knew, he was saying 'good-by ', without uttering a word. Her heart ached, as she softly cried into the hollow of his neck. All he could do, was to hold her close while kissing her tears away.

Later, as they headed back to the beach house, their arms around each other, Drew spoke softly against her hair. "I love you Gail, I have from the moment I first saw you,....and I'll never forget the happiness, and love we've shared here on this island. It will last me all the days of my life. In time, there will be another man in your life"....Drew, held his breath for a moment, then in a steady voice, he continued talking. "A man that can give you all the things a woman needs, love, a home, and children. You need a husband and lover that you'll never be ashamed of. These are the things I could never give you. Forgive me darling." His voice had suddenly become husky, and he had to clear his throat, and draw in a deep breath, before he could go on. Gail tried to interrupt him, saying, "No never!" But, he silenced her with his finger tips against her lips.

"Your very special to me, and I'll always remember the day's we've spent here together." He ran his finger tips along the edge of her chin, and felt her soft lips as he spoke softly, "Did you know, that before we ever make love, I called this the "Island of Dreams ", because.....I did nothing but day-dream about you? I'm glad I made love to you, because...my dreams were nothing compared to loving you. You'll always be in my heart."

'No! It can't end like this!...I won't let it!' Gail threw her arms around him, and looked up through teary eyes, "Drew, please don't let it end like this! I need and love you...Please!" The tears that she had tried to hold back, slowly weld up in her eyes, and spilled over, only to slide down her face. "Please darling, write or call me!"

He pulled her in close to his heart, as he whispered into her hair, "No, I can't do that. Oh Gail darling don't cry....please! Can't you see how hard it is for me to let you go? If there were any way that I could keep you with me....I would." His voice became husky, as he pleaded, "Please darling, be brave, for I need all of your strength right now."

"Drew...I'll always love you, and if you ever need me, I'll be here, waiting for you, on our 'Island of Dreams."

He looked down at her lovely face once more, then bent his head, to kiss those lovely lips for the last time, then he turned and walked away into the night.

Gail sat up in bed, unable to sleep, aching for her lover, who would never be hers, when she heard the helicopter winding up. Now she knew why Drew had been so late for the cookout! He must have packed, and had everything put in the chopper before he saw her. Jumping out of bed, she ran to the door, throwing it open, as she ran out into the yard, and yelled up at the helicopter as it flew by, "Don't go!...Drew, I love you!!...Come back!" Sobbing, as if she were being torn apart, she turned and stumbled back into the house, where she threw herself into the first chair that she bumped into. There she cried herself to sleep.

Gail, woke to the sound of the surf, and found herself on the couch, where she had collapsed the night before. She did nothing but walk around and cry all day. Everywhere she looked, she could see Drew walking along the beach, or tossing her into the water, while the moonlight played on their bodies. The night was the worst, she longed for the feel of his body pressed close to hers, to feel his strong arms around her, and to hear the trembling of his voice, when he was deep inside her. God!....She needed him in her life! In her heart, she knew that she would never love another man as she loved Drew. He was her first love,...and he'd be her last one,........anyway......who said, she couldn't be an old maid if she wanted to!!

To-day, Bill would be coming to pick her up. The island wasn't the same without Drew, and she was glad to be going home. She was still crying, as she packed the last of her bags. She took one last look around, and promised herself that she wouldn't cry in front of Bill. Wiping her nose and brushing the tears from her face, she bent and picked up the last of her bags, and carried them down to the landing, for...she didn't want to remember anyone, but Drew, being on the island with her.

As the cabin cruiser slowly pulled away from the island, Bill, looked at the young lady who stood with her back to him, and shook his head. She was all tanned up, but the smile was gone from her eyes, and she was like one who didn't care whether she lived, or died.

Too bad, he thought, most of the people who leave the island, had come to better terms with themselves by the time they were to leave. The rest of the journey was in dead silence, as Gail stayed below deck.

Gail, was tired and drained of all emotion when she was greeted at the dock, by Donna and Paul, who looked at each other in dismay, as Gail, hugged them both, then turned and walked to the car in silence.

All the way to Gail's apartment they tried to get her to talk about her vacation, but all they got out of her was..." Yes, it was beautiful, and yes, she liked the island, and yes she was glad to be home." Once inside Gail's apartment, she turned to the two people who meant so much in her life hugging them, and asked if they wouldn't mind leaving as she was really bushed.

When Donna kissed her sister good-night, she noticed the look on her face, as if she were ready to cry. Paul, saw a very depressed and sick girl. Being a doctor, he knew, he had to do something about it.....and fast! He had hoped that this vacation would have spruced her up, but it had back fired badly! As he bent to kiss Gail's cheek, he noticed that she was running a fever. Jokingly, he said, "Why don't you take two aspirin, and go to bed."

"Thanks Doc, I will," she answered, very close to tears. After closing the door behind them, Gail leaned against it and cried. "Oh God...how can I stand not knowing what's happening to him?" Being a nurse, she knew that more surgery was indicated,..but how much,...and when, and whether or not he would permit it, these were the questions that she had no answers for.

Gail, suddenly realized that she knew very little about him. Where he lived, or what he did for a living was a mystery to her. She knew, in her heart that she would never see him again. She had gambled on their love hoping that he would change his mind.

He would have to come to her, or he would never except her love, as anything but pity. She had gambled on love.......and lost........tomorrow, she would try to pick up the pieces of her life, and go on.......but ....not tonight! Tonight she needed him....but he would only be there in her memories for the rest of her life......

Drew ran and stumbled, as he raced to where the helicopter was ready and waiting for him. He was out of breath, and as he climbed into the seat, his eyes blurred, as he cried out in his anger, "Why Me!...God!...Why Me!...Why didn't you just let me die!?" Then a sob broke out from his throat, and he cried for the one thing that had come to mean so much to him,....Gail. Without her, his dreams of a home, children and everything else that was worth living for, were lost forever.

He knew there was no turning back now. He kept telling himself over and over, that one look of fright, or pity in her eyes would kill him. This was the hand that he was delt, and he had to play it out alone.

As he passed over the beach house, he gulped back the lump in his throat, as he watched Gail run out the front door and raise her arms to him. 'Good-bye my love," he whispered, as his throat tightened up, leaving him speechless. Seconds later, the island was out of sight and he was headed for the mainland.

Drew, had been back a couple of weeks when he received a call from Phil, asking him to come into the office as soon as possible. As he drove his pick-up truck into the parking lot at the burn center, Drew looked over at the red Camero that was parked beside him. Getting out of the cab, he ran his fingers over the hood saying, "I'll own one like you someday." Then he proceeded to walk through the main entrance to the hospital, and on up to the main desk. He pulled in his breath as he gave the receptionist his name, and took a seat. Soon he was told to go in that the doctor would see him now.

Philip, got up from his chair and greeted Drew, with a smile and a hearty hand shake. "Take a chair, Drew. Tell me, did you have a good stay at the beach house?"

"Sure, don't I always? It's everything you said it was doc, and even more."

"I just love the place, but the wife and I can't seem to get away often enough."

Leaning forward, his elbows resting on his knees, his fingers tightly entwined with each other, he asked, "Doc, do you let many people use your place?"

"Yes, quite often. Whenever I have a patient that needs something I can't give them, I usually send them there for a few weeks. Sometimes it pays off,....and other times it backfires, I'm sorry to say."

Staring at Drew, and trying to read his mind, he continued to speak. "I thought that when I sent you there, you would come back rested and ready for another go at surgery,...but...you look down about something. I figured that when you returned, I'd give you the green light, but now I don't know. Do you feel ready for this? Remember, this is the big one. You'll be in bandages for a few weeks, and it will be rough. After that, two or three minor adustments, and you should be a new man.

In his heart, Drew really didn't care any longer, how he looked, but he had come this far, so why not get on with it? "Yes....I'm ready. Where do I sign, and when do we start?" His hands were beginning to sweat, as he realized what he was about to go through.

"How about the day after tomorrow? At 3:30 you can check in."

"O.K. Doc, see you then." As Drew was about to leave, Doc, shook his hand and clapped him on the back, saying, "Don't worry, everything will be fine." "Ya...I know Doc...Thanks."

When Drew got to his truck, he noticed that the red Camero was gone. Oh well...that was the story of his life. He'd fall for someone or something and then it would be gone in a flash.

As he drove back to his pad, he knew he had a lot of loose ends to finish up before Wednesday. He knew his buddy Al, could handle any charter flights that might come in. As for Nancy, she could handle the office with great style. Nothing got past her, so between the two of them he decided he didn't have a thing to worry about.

He made himself a drink then went and sat in the big arm chair by the window. As he sat staring out at the sky, he could see Gail's beautiful face staring back at him. He needed her badly,...right now,...this minute, just to have her arms around him, would chase all his fears away.

Drew, knew he had to psyche himself up to go through with this surgery, for deep down he was terrified. What if something went wrong, and he was left worse off then he was now? He didn't even want to think of it. With that, he downed the glass of liquor in one large swallow. It burned going down, and his eyes tearing for the moment, but it gave him just enough courage to hang on.

If that turned out to be the case, he knew what he had to do.......Hell.......many helicopters crashed into mountains. This he could do. He had cut himself off from the only loving thing that he adored, so why worry about it? To die.....was a piece of cake.

CHAPTER THREE

Monday morning, Gail reported to Dr.Wild's office,before she could resume her duties on the ward. After he had examined her, he asked if anything disturbing had taken place over the last two weeks. She lied, flatly saying," No."

Dr. Wild, didn't like the way she looked or talked. It was like she had put a shield around herself. Sensing something was definitely bothering her he decided to discuss Gail with both Philip and Paul later.

Getting up and walking toward the door, Gail asked, "Can I go now?" Her hand was tightly squeezing the door handle as she waited for his answer. "Yes, but check back with me in two weeks."

"Is that an order?!" She snapped.

"Yes…consider it one." His tone had changed and she knew he was upset with her. Without a backward glance she left,….closing the door behind her.

Minutes later as she entered the ward, she couldn't help but smile as everyone was glad to see her back. There was so much to do, that the day flew by and suddenly it was the end of her shift.

Once she entered her apartment, she fell apart. No matter how hard she tried, she couldn't get Drew out of her mind, or her heart. She couldn't sleep and the night dragged by. Toward dawn, she finally fell asleep with his name on her lips, only to wake up and reach out and touch the empty bed beside her.

The days flew by as Gail put all of her energy into her work. She stayed later at the hospital just so her evenings at home would be shorter. If she was tired enough she would be able to sleep. Other times she would ly awake tormented by visions of being in Drew's arms, always touching and whispering little phrases of love that she desperately wanted to hear. Then without warning, she would cry out in her sleep only to wake up in a cold sweat with her heart beating wildly inside her chest.

Gail was on her coffee break, when Paul came into the lounge.

"Gail, You're just the person I've been looking for," he said, as he pulled up a chair beside her. "I hear you've been staying late after your shift.

We"re short handed and I have a patient who needs a little extra care for a few days."

Gail thought that she was in for a lecture, for staying after her shift was over,but now as she looked at her brother-in-laws face, and listening to him, she realized that this patient meant a great deal to him. Suddenly, she was listening to every word that Paul was saying. "He's had some rather extensive reconstruction work done on his face, and I know he could use a friend about now.....and a little conversation, even though he can't answer you. Most of his face will be bandaged, except for the usual openings. He's going to feel insecure for a while.....so that's where you come in to the picture."

"I know," spoke up Gail as she smiled at him, "you want me to hold his hand and take his mind off his pain."

"Will you do this for me? He's a personal friend of mine, and he has no one." Gail could feel how much Paul cared for this man and she knew by the tone of his voice, that he was worried about his welfare. "I think you're just what he needs." Paul had taken her hand into his, as he waited for an answer.

"Sure Paul, anything for you. What's his name and what room is he in?"

"We call him Pappy, and I think he'll feel more comfortable if you call him that. He's in room 213. Just drop in when ever you can. Paul leaned down and kissed his sister-in-law on the cheek, saying, "Thanks honey, I knew I could count on you." then he turned and left. Hearing the relief in Paul's voice Gail smiled,and was glad to be able to help his friend.

It was five-thirty when Gail looked at her watch. Her shift was over and she called, "Good-night" to her patients as she headed for the corridor. As she started out the door, she suddenly remembered her promise to Paul. Going back into the hospital, she headed for the elevator and to the second floor. On the way up, she decided to pick up something to eat on the way home.

As Gail turned the handle and stept into room 213, she noticed the patient lying very still. 'He's probably sleeping' she thought, so she quietly sat down beside the bed and watched for any motion, indicating that he was conscious.

As she looked at him lying there so still, swathed in bandages, it was hard to tell just how old he was. He had a large frame and a well toned body, by the way his arms and chest seemed to strain against the hospital gown he had on. Getting up she checked his intravenous, to be sure it was working properly, and took his pulse from force of habit. When she touched his wrist, he made a little moaning sound and moved his other hand,as if to touch his face.

Quickly, she took hold of his hand, telling him not to touch his face at all. She told him, she knew it must be frightening for him not to be able to talk or see, but that she was there, and between the regular nurses and herself, they would help him all they could.

Gail told him to put his left hand up and down for yes, and sideways for no. This way she could talk to him and at least he could let her know whether or not he was in any pain.

"Dr. Miles, told me you two are good friends and you're name is Pappy, at least that's what he calls you, so… if you don't mind I'll call you that too."

His hand went up and down twice. "Good!" Gail answered, as she touched his hand, so he would know that she had seen his hand signal. "I have a nick name too, so I'll use it with you, if you promise not to tell anyone." She laughed as she said, 'High Pockets, I was given that name in the Navy. Now only my closest friends call me that." Then she asked, "Are you in pain?" He signaled, no. "Are you thirsty?" This time his hand moved up and down rapidly, signaling yes! Load and clear.

"I'll get you a drink," she then lifted the glass of water up to his lips, placing the straw carefuly into the hole that was provided for his mouth. He gulped in the water, like a man dying of thirst. "Not too much this time, Pappy," she warned him, as she took the straw out of his mouth.

"Try to sleep now…I'll stay with you until you doze off, and yes, I'll be back here tomorrow, and when ever I get a chance to drop in during the day." As she patted his arm for reasurence, he took hold of her hand and clasped it tightly in his own, as if to say, "Thanks."

Gail sat holding his hand in her's until his breathing slowed down, and his hand lost it's grip on her's, as he fell into a sound sleep.

"Sleep well, my friend," she whispered, as she left closing the door softly behind her.

Gail, drove to the nearest drive-in and got something to eat. She was finishing the last french- fry as she pulled into the parking lot where she lived. It had been a long day but she was glad that she had dropped in on Pappy. She had a sense of feeling warm and alive for the first time since her return home.

After taking a long hot shower and putting on her night-gown, she sat on the edge of the bed, then it came to her, that she hadn't thought of Drew for the last nine hours. Could she be getting over him? No! Never in a million years.

She asked herself, over and over again, why couldn't Pappy be Drew! Then she could be with him, to love and care for him. "Oh Drew," she cried out into the night, "Where are you tonight, when I need you so desperately." It was after two in the morning when Gail stopped tossing and turning and finally fell asleep.

The following day when Drew stirred, he could hear his friends, Dr.Paul and Dr. Philip talking. Sensing that he was awake, they told him not to move his head, and to try and lay quietly for a few days.

"Pappy, you did real well," Dr. Philip, told him. "You'll be in a little discomfort for a few days, but we'll try to keep the pain down to a minimum. Do you understand me?" Seeing Pappy move his hand in a gesture saying, "Yes." Philip, laughed saying, "I see you've already had a visit from our favorite nurse, High-pocket's. Don't ever tell her that I called her that. She, thinks that Dr.Paul, is the only one who knows her nick name."

Dr. Paul, laughingly said, "Pappy, if you could see her, you'd know why. She has it all in the right places." After checking out Drew, the two doctors left, leaving him to think over all that had happened to him in the last forty-eight hours.

Drew, barely remembered a sweet voice telling him to rest and that she would stay with him for a while. He remembered a comforting hand that some how calmed him down.

As the days past, Drew had pleanty of time to remember Gail, and the island. When ever the pain got too bad, or his temper would flare up, he'd remember how she felt in his arms, how her lips pressed against his. He could almost feel her beside him now. God, how he wanted and needed her! He heard the sound of things ratteling on a tray and he knew he was no longer alone with his thoughts.

Whatever they gave him through a straw, tasted terrible but his body was crying out for food and it was either that or intravenous alone. So he drank it and tried to make a noise, so that the nurse would know that he hated it. But, she would only laugh and say, "Drink it, I know it's terrible tasting but soon you'll be able to eat real food again."

Drew, had dozed off, when he was awakened by someone putting on a light. He, wanted to ask who it was, but all he could do was raise his hand to say, 'Hello'.

"Hi, I see your awake!" There it was again that wonderful voice, he suddenly, realized just how much he was beginning to depend on this nurse. She seemed to know what he was going through with out him telling her. "I thought I'de drop in to see how you were doing." Then she asked, "Did you drink all your dinner?"

Drew, raised his hand in a definite manner meaning, "Yes!"

"I'll see if I can get you some juice or a soda. Would you like that?" 'Yes', he motioned, as he thought,' High - Pocket's, you and I are going to get along fine!'

A few minutes later she returned with the best tasting Coke he had ever tasted! As he sipped it,she remarked," It's so quiet in here. How about if I put the telivision on? I'll mention a few things, and you can hold up your fingers as to which one you want to hear. O.K." Here goes.....Rock music, soft music, or the football game?"

He could have kissed her when she mentioned the football game. He quickly held up three fingers. "Great," she laughed, "I love football too!"

Then he heard a chair being pulled up near his bed, and he knew she was going to stay for a while.

"Pappy, when this is all over, and your out of here, if you can tear yourself away from the ladies for a day, I'de like to treat you to a football game. We could have a cold beer and a hot dog or two, and I'll try not to embarrass you by yelling too loud!"

She laughed as she talked, and her laughter made him forget the ordeal that was coming up soon. The bandages were to be removed, and the doctor's had promised him that he would be able to eat real food again, but his eyes and the left side of his face would still be covered with bandages, for a few more weeks. Just to be able to eat was enough to make him happy. He had a million questions to ask High-Pockets, but that too would have to wait.

"Well Pappy," yawned Gail, I have to call it a night. It was a hectic day on the ward and I'm so tired that if I don't leave now, I'll have to move you over and crash here for the night. Now you don't want that, do you?" There she was laughing again. He wanted to smile back at her, but all he could do was wave,' Good-by.'

All the way home, Gail wondered why no one ever came to visit this man who seemed to be of a gently nature. He was better than most patients, usually they threw their glasses, and tried to knock the bed pans away, or found

61

things to throw onto the floor, out of aggrevation, I guess I'll have to have a talk with Paul.

Later that night, alone in her bed,in the darkened room she thought about Drew, and she could almost feel his presence in the room. 'Where are you tonight?' She whispered into the night, 'I need to know if your all right, please God, make him come back to me.' Rolling over, she hugged her pillow to her as she knew this was going to be another night of crying into her pillow, only to rise in the morning with red puffy eyes, for all the world to see.

Saturday was Gail's day off, and she was vacuming the rug when the phone rang. When she answered it, she smiled, as it was her sister Donna, on the other end of the line.

"Hi Gail, how about coming over for dinner and a few drinks tonight? I won't take no for an answer. We havn't seen of heard from you in two weeks."

"I know Donna. I've been busy at the hospital and I've been dropping in on a friend of Pauls, so by the time I get home I barely get cleaned up and into bed I go."

"Well, I think it's about time you broke the routine. Come over early, so we can talk........Remember EARLY!"

"Alright Donna, I'll be there around five. I've got to clean the apartment and then I want to pick up a few things down-town, then I'll be over. Thanks for the invite!'

"Bye Gail, see you later."

As the telephone clicked, Gail put the receiver down and started to clean again, only this time she did it with a purpose. She would have to hurry if she wanted to do everything before five.

When the house work was finished, she threw off her old jeans and sweat-shirt, and headed for the shower. The warm water felt great as it ran down over her body, relaxing her.

As she washed herself, she remembered how Drew's hands had traveled over her skin, when they had gone skinny-dipping. She closed her eyes for a moment, and pretended that her hands were Drew's. 'Oh Drew,.... are you feeling someone else's body now?' This thought brought her back to reality, and she quickly washed her hair then stept out of the shower. While drying off, she noticed that she had lost weight. Maybe a little too much. She couldn't afford to go out and buy a new wardrobe, so she had better keep a check on her weight.

She, finally decided on a soft green cotton dress, and silver earings, that were a gift from Mexico. They were large hoops, but she loved them. After placing a silver chain around her neck the dress looked great. She took extra pains with her hair and makeup, as she didn't want to get a nother lecture from her sister about her appearence. After stepping into her brown heels, she grabbed her leather jacket and bag off the chair, and stopped to look at herself one more time in the full length mirror.

What she saw looking back at her was a tall, thin nicely rounded woman with a smile on her face, all except for her eyes. They were sad eyes and even with the help of green mascara, she couldn't hide the heartache that was plain to see. She stood back and took one more look before she turned and hurried toward the door.

While she was in the department store, she decided to get Pappy a gift, as he had become more than a patient to her, some how she thought of him as a friend, and wanted to cheer him up. She, decided on a pair of soft cotton pajamas and a matching robe. She, had noticed that every time Pappy, had gotten out of bed he felt self conscious in the hospital attire. After the pajamas were gift wrapped, she hurried out of the store,as it was getting late and she wanted to spend an hour or so with Pappy.

With this in mind, she backed her red Camero out of the parking lot and headed for the hospital. Minutes later she pulled into the parking lot with a squeal of breaks, that would wake the dead! Laughing, to herself as she got out of the car, she patted the hood saying, "Well now you've had your first run with a stock car driver!" Imagin going sixty in a thirty mile an hour zone!

As she walked threw the hospital corridors, doctor's and nurse's, as well as patients that she knew, told her that she looked terrific. One doctor even called her beautiful. When she poked her head into the children's ward to say hello, she was thrilled to see their reaction. Never had anyone at the hospital ever seen her out of uniform. When little David, told her she was beautiful, she bent down and kissed him saying, "Thanks little man, you've made my day!"

Suddenly she felt great, as if someone had lifted a weight off her shoulders. Why, she even felt pretty as she hurried toward room 213 with a smile on her face. She could see Pappy, sitting in the patient's lounge as she walked down the hall. She suddenly realized that her heels were making little clicking sounds, that Pappy could hear. He turned around to face her as she approached him.

"Hi Pappy, I brought you a present." she told him as she smiled down at him.

He, held up his hands, as if to say," No!"

"Listen buster," she said stearnly, "I don't go around buying men gifts, so just take it and wear it on Monday, your big day."

How could he refuse, when her tone of voice told him so much. She had spunk, and she reminded him of someone else he knew, that could hold her ground when she wanted to.

High-Pockets, walked him back to his room, and on the way, he touched her jacket, and made a jesture like...." Wow, nice coat." She picked up on it and described how she was dressed, and that she was going to her sister's house for dinner. She found herself telling him how she hadn't been out for so long, and that she felt great,, just to be dressed up and going somewhere beside the hospital and home.

As Drew, listened to her talk, he sensed a change in her. Some times her voice sounded like she was far away........but today.....she was alive and bubbling over. He opened his gift with her help, and he made all kinds of funny noises to let her know how pleased he was.

He reached for her hand, and held it a minute between his two large gentle hands. They both were quiet for a minute, and Gail wondered why his hands holding her's disturbed her so. Releasing her hand from his, she spoke up abruptly, with difficulty, "I have to leave now, or I'll be late for dinner. I'll see you tomorrow, By Pappy."

She, had turned and left, but her perfume lingered, filling the room with her presence. 'God! he thought.....what a woman! She, had known that he hated the hospital robes and everything else he was told to wear.' Lifting the robe out of the box, he put it on and could tell by the smoothness of it that it was expensive. High-Pockets, had told him they were dark blue ..... 'not bad taste' he thought.

Feeling the soft material, his thoughts went back to the night when he had sat across from Gail, in the dark, and she had worn a white satin robe. He, could still see her chest rising and falling, with every breath she took,making the satin mold around her breast's which stirred his manhood, even now, as he thought of her, he could feel himself hardening. He groaned, as his need for her was tearing him apart. 'God damn it Gail,' He thought, 'I don't even know were you live ....or... what you do for a living! I wouldn't talk about myself to you,and I didn't want to know to much about you at the time, for fear I'd weaken and call you. Oh darling, I wish I could speak to you now, just to know that your alright.' He hit his fists against the bed in his agony. Never to see, or touch her again,drove all the life out of him. What did anything in life matter now,....now that she was lost to him forever.

After dinner, Gail and Donna, sat side- by- side on the couch while Paul made them another drink. As he passed Gail her drink, he asked with concern, "How do you like my friend Pappy?"

Gail, told him what a great patient he was, but that she knew that deep down he had fears and doubts about the outcome of his surgery. She, then told him of the gift that she had bought for him and how he had reacted when he received it.

"Good!" Paul replied, "Thats just what he needs right now, a friend to lean on." Then he sat down opposite Gail, he continued to speak of his friend. "Pappy, has isolated himself from everyone since his injury. His only close friends that I know of are Al, his co-pilot, and Nancy, a middle aged woman who is his secretary, and girl Friday."

"Is he a pilot?" asked Gail, with intrest.

"Ya, he flies helicopters. He has his own private business. Al, is holding down the fort for him, while he's here. Al and Pappy, were in the service together. When Pappy's able to talk, he'll probably tell you all kinds of tales."

Gail, sipped on her drink, as her thoughts went back to the island, and another helicopter pilot, that she loved.

"Gail! Where were you just then? You didn't hear a word I was saying. Paul and I, want to hear all about your stay on the island. The real story this time! We know something happened to make you so miserable, but seeing you were alone, it rules out a man."

"Maybe I wasn't alone," she answered, just above a whisper, as she played with the stem of her wine glass. "Yes, It's a man," she confessed, "We met, spent a few days together, fell in love......and then he left me." Her eyes filled with tears, as she took a large gulp of her drink.

"Oh Gail, I'm sorry," whispered Donna as she leaned over and put her arm around her sister. "What made him leave you, if he loves you? Is he married?"

"No," nodded Gail, not being able to talk through the tears that fell freely now.

Paul, was glad to see her cry, to finally rellease all the pent up emotion that she had been carrying around inside her for so long. Now, maybe he could help her. Reaching out and taking her by the hand, he asked, "Why did he leave?" His heart went out to her, for he knew if Donna ever left him, he would be lost forever, for he was very much in love with his wife.

"Oh Paul," Gail blurted out,between deep breaths and silent tears, that she kept wiping away with the back of her hand, "when I first met him, he was so mysterious that I thought he was a criminal, and that he didn't want me to reconize him. He never let me see him in the daylight. Only when it was dark in a room or at night. We argued terribly at first, and I almost hated him, until I found out the reason why he wouldn't let me see him. His face is badly disfigured by burns and lacerations, and when I saw this, I was shocked but I still loved him." She, began to cry softly as if her heart would break.

"Did he know, that you knew his secret?" asked Paul,softly.

"No, I couldn't tell him, I...I knew he'de disappear. He would think I was pitying him."

"Didn't you tell him that you were a nurse, and that it didn't matter to you?"

"No....He knows nothing about me or where I come from. I know little about him except for his name,.... Drew Hatfield, and the love we shared. We were practically strangers, but our love for each other was real."

Hugging Gail closer to her, Donna asked tenderly, "How do you know that' it's real love that you feel for this man, and not pity? You've helped so many burn victims.....be honest with yourself."

"Oh Donna, I'm so miserable," she sobbed, into her sister's shoulder, "we made love, and it was beautiful.... as long as I couldn't see his face, we were in heaven. he has to be the one to find me. Can you understand that? .....If he realy loves me, he'll find me, and when he does.....I'll be there waiting for him. What realy hurts, is not knowing where he is, or what's happening to him."

After Gail, had left for home, Paul looked at Donna, saying," God in heaven, she's in love with Pappy, and doesn't even know that it's him she's been helping!"

"How could she know! She only knows him by his nick name, and she has never seen his face, or heard his voice, since he's been there! She's in love with a man named Drew......Not Pappy! They are one in the same person! Oh Paul, what will happen when Gail finds out?"

"I don't know honey.... my main concern right now is how he will take it. Remember, as a nurse, she's seen him at his worst. If he surmises it at all, he can't let anyone know until he's able to talk."

"When will that be?"

"Soon......Monday, we'll change the dressing's for the first time. He, won't be able to open his eyes, but he'll have the freedom of his chin and mouth, so he can speak to her. I just don't know what's going to happen."

Paul, paced back and forth, running his fingers through his hair trying to think, for he was concerned for both his sister-in-law, and his patient. Knowing both of them, he had to agree that they would be good for each other. And yes...Pappy, would have to be the one to pick up the relationship, if he wanted it badly enough.

"Oh Paul, what will happen to them?" asked Donna, as tears sprang to her eyes.

"Seeing her tears, Paul, pulled her into his arms and held her tightly as he spoke, softly into her hair," I can arrange it so Gail will be there when the first bandages come off. She'll, have to read his medical chart where she'll see his given name. After that, it will be up to her. Later, I'll have a talk with her, then we'll just have to wait and see what developes."

He, held Donna close, while she cried for the two lovers, who may never know the joy of being together as man and wife. She burried her head into his shoulder, and hugged him fiercely to her, as she shed tears for her sister, whom she loved dearly.

Monday morning was finally here, and as Drew sat waiting for the doctor's, he realized that he was scared stiff of what may be lying underneath the bandages. He, had hoped that High Pockets, would be there for moral support. He had begun to depend on this wonderful nurse for so many things. Then as the door opened, he was brought back to reality.

Doctor Philip, was the first one to speak, going closer to where Drew was sitting, he placed his hand on his arm, saying, "Morning Pappy, are you ready for the unveiling?"

"Let's wait a few more minutes,Phil," interrupted Paul," I think High Pockets, wanted to be in on this."

All Drew could think of was that she had kept her promise to be there. He, drew in a deep breath, and let out a sigh, that was picked up by both doctors, as they looked at each other over Drew's head. Paul. had filled Philip in on the situation between Drew and Gail, and they were prepared for the worst.

The door opened and Gail entered the room. "Sorry I'm late doctor's," she apoligized. Then going to Pappy, she layed her hand on his shoulder, saying, "How's it going? Are you ready?"

He, signaled in a manner, answering yes, as he held her hand for a moment. Then he released it, and turned his attention to the doctors.

As Gail, released Drew's sweaty hand, she realized just how scared he was, and her heart went out to him.

"O.k....Let's get on with it." There was anxiety in Doctor Paul's voice, as he spoke.

"Nurse, take notes as I speak. The chart is on the table near the bed," Paul said, as he looked over at Philip.

"Yes Doctor."

As Gail, picked up the medical chart, she could hear the clipping of scissors, as the bandages were being removed. She looked up, as the bandages were lifted off, except for two covering his eyes.

She wrote with haste as the doctors talked. They kept telling Pappy, to keep his eyes closed. That things looked real good, and if he wanted to, he could have a drink, and then try to talk.

As Gail, wrote the last few statements, she was curious as to what Pappy's, real name was. When she read Drew Hatfield, she let out a little gasp, and drew in her breath. The doctor's looked at her, as she covered her mouth, and tears sprang to her eyes, only to run silently down her face.

Pappy, sensing something was wrong, quickly asked, in a terrified voice, "Doc, what's wrong with my face!?" "High Pockets, tell me the truth!……..For God sakes, someone tell me!!" The pleading in his voice was more than she could bear. Gail, quickly took Drew's hand in her's squeezing it tightly, as she managed to get control of ferself. "I guess I got a little carried away. I always cry when it's good news, and I've let myself get involved with a patient. Everything is perfect!" Then she asked, "Haven't you ever heard anyone cry for joy?"

Drew, swallowed hard, as he managed to speak above the lumpin his throat, "No…..never for me."

The doctor's worked fast, talking all the while, to assure Drew, that when the swelling and redness disappeared he'd be as good as new. At the same time they kept an eye on Gail, as she had turned white as a ghost, and looked like she was getting ready to run at any moment.

Pull yourself together Gail kept telling herself, he needs me as a friend right now, and nothing more…..With that in mind, she sponged off the upper part of Pappy, and helped him into his pajama top, saying "Perhaps you would like to get into the bottoms." With that she led him to the adjoining bathroom. Once the bathroom door closed behind him, Gail, turned and glared at the two doctor's, "Why? ….Why didn't you tell me!?"

Paul quickly went to her, "I didn't know until the other night, when you mentioned his name. No one knew he was on the island, not even Philip! Please Gail," he pleaded, "play this out for a while, it means a lot to Pappy, to have you as a friend, Remember.....he only knows you as High Pockets!"

Before she could answer, the bathroom door opened, and there stood Pappy, waiting for her. He, had a smile on his face, and standing there he looked wonderful to her. 'How could I have missed it,' it's really him! She wanted to throw her arms around him and hold him close to her heart, but she knew it was impossible. Instead, she took him by the arm and helped him back to his bed.

"Try and rest now Pappy, and we'll drop in on you later," the doctor's told him, as they left the room.

"High-Pockets, have they gone?"

"Yes, now try and get some sleep."

"I will, but first I have something to say to you. I never would have made it this far, if it hadn't been for you. I just want to thank you for everything. ....I wanted to thank you for so many things, but not being able to talk, it was impossible. Thanks again nurse, your a real friend."

As Gail, puffed up his pillow, she had to lean over him and it took all of her will power not to pull him into her arms, to feel him close to her for just a moment. When she started to straighten up, he grabbed her hand, and gently brought it to his lips and kissed it.

Gail, drew her hand away and pressed it to her lips, to keep from crying out, as she turned and fled the room.

That night as she sat curled up on the couch, the phone rang, knowing it would be Paul, she answered it, after it rang a few times. "Hello Gail, are you all right? Look

72

honey, if you need to talk....I'm here. Have you decided what you are going to do about Drew?"

"Paul, I really don't know. I've been sitting here thinking. He needs me as a nurse, as well as a friend.......as High Pockets. So.... that's what I'll be for now, just a friend. I'll think of some excuse before the bandages are to be removed from his eyes. I know, he'd hate me if he knew it was me all along I know he wouldn't believe me now, even if I told him that I didn't know who he was. I'm just glad he had the surgery. "Then there was a long silence and Paul, asked, "Gail! Are you still there?" "Yes...oh Paul, he's so damn good looking, she said, with a lump in her throat," he'll forget all about the girl he met on his "Island of Dreams" as he called it." Hearing her voice quivering as she talked, broke his heart, for he knew the heartache she was feeling. "Please Paul, don't let him know that it's me! I love him so ... I just want to see him well and happy."

"But Gail, can you do this, can you stand to see him every day, then just walk away?! Are you strong enough for that?"

"Yes Paul, I can do anything for Drew, for I love him more than life it self. I can't talk any more just now," she whispered, as the tears started again.

"Goodnight Gail, we love you."

As the phone clicked, she placed the receiver back in it's cradle and hugged the couch pillow to her breast as she cried out in her agony,

"God help me to be strong!"

The next few weeks flew by, as the time for Drew's bandages to come off grew near, Gail, had started to leave the hospital earlier than usual in order to leave without seeing Drew. She hadn't seen Drew, in two days and she missed him terribly. She was sick inside thinking of not being there when the bandages were to be moved. She just couldn't take a chance of being reconized. Each day, she tried to put him out of her mind, as she threw all her energy into her work in the childrens ward, which left her exausted by nightfall.

Drew, wondered why High Pockets, hadn't been in to see him for the last few days. He had asked about her but no one seemed to know who he was talking about. Then he decided to ask Dr. Philip, he in return, told him that she was busy on her ward and that she had quite a knack with her (kid's), as she called them. Yes, he could understand that, for hadn't she been gentle with him, yet stern when he needed it, but most of all, she had become his friend, and he didn't want to loose that friendship.

Later that day, a young volunteer came in to ask him if he would like to take a walk, Drew jumped at the offer. "Look, could you take me down to the childrens ward, and seat me where no one can see me, but that I can hear them? "he asked, hopefully.

"Sure, and I'll come back for you later, Do you mind if I ask why?"

"No, I owe you that much. The nurse on the ward is a friend of mine, and I hear that she is great with the kids, and I just wanted to hear it for myself. I don't want to embarass her, so if she doesn't see me there, it would be great."

"O.k. Pappy, let's go!" Drew smiled, as the young girl took hold of his arm. Soon he was seated just outside the childrens ward, behind a curtain where he could hear everything, but could not be seen.

The children were giggling and talking, and he could hear High Pockets, laughing and fooling with them. He couldn't help but smile as he listened. Then suddenly, with out warning, he heard a child cry out in pain, and the hairs on the back of his neck stood up, and he broke out in a cold sweat!

Memories, came flooding back.........memories, that he tried to forget. Memories of how he had cried out in agony, when his helicopter had crashed, and later at the hospital, as doctors, tried to put his face back together.

Then, there was that voice again, talking softly to the child, and soothing it's fears and pain, by what sounded like a rocking chair, and a lullaby being sung softly. Suddenly, he noticed that the other children had stopped talking and were quiet also, as if knowing the pain, that the other child was suffering. He felt a tear slide down his face, as he realized what a wonderful woman this High Pockets, really was. How strong she was, to be able to handle so much pain and sorrow, and to be able to show so much love for them all, with out breaking down herself.

When he was back in his own room, he sat thinking about Gail, and the island. If only he had the guts, and the nerve like this nurse, he would crawl back to Gail, and beg her forgiveness, forever thinking that he could live without her!

While Pappy, was eating his supper, High Pockets, dropped in to say,hello. Pappy stopped eating, and smiled in her direction, over joyed at hearing her cheerfull voice again, "Hi pal,....where have you been keeping yourself? I've missed you dropping in."

"I've been busy lately, and there aren't enough hour's in the day. Doc. tells me, their going to remove the bandages, and that's good news."

"Ya....then I'll be able to get out of here for a few weeks. Then I'll be coming back for the last touch-up's as the Doc calls it." He tried to laugh it off, but his laugh didn't ring true.

Gail's eyes were glued to his lips, and his smile was worth seeing. She kept remembering how his lips had felt, when he had kissed her, how she felt the smoothness of his teeth, as her tongue had searched his mouth for the taste of him. Oh God!..How she wanted to be kissed by those lips just once more. "That's true," she heard herself saying, "The worst will be over, and you can pick up where you left off."

"What are your plans for the future? You never talk about yourself. Is there a man in your life?"

"I have no plans right now....I have a vacation coming up and I guess I'll take it and get away for a while. As for a gentelman friend...I don't know. There was a man." she said, with a heavy heart," he left me for reasons of his own,....I'll always love him, but he has to want me enough to come back on his own."

Drew, could tell by her voice that she must love this man deeply, and that she was trying hard not to cry. "God, High Pockets, I'm sorry to hear that. He's a damn fool, who ever he is, to let a great woman like you get away! Why....I could fall in love with you myself, but I gave my heart once....and I have nothing left for anyone else. I still love her...but she's out of my reach forever."

She, could see how hard it was for him to keep his self control, the same as she. Backing up to the door, she whispered back over her shoulder, "Maybe...if we wish real hard, our dreams of love will come true."

As the door closed softly behind her, Drew, was left alone with his memories of Gail, on his "Island of Dreams."

Both doctor's realized that Gail was suffering from a broken heart, and that Drew, was showing signs of it too. They both felt that they were to blame, as it had been their idea for Gail to stay on the island in the first place. They thought,by the time Gail arrived, Drew would be gone. Little did they realize, that having a helicopter at his disposal, Drew could drop in anytime, as he knew where Philip kept the spare key. It was nothing for Drew to fly down and spend a day or two. To Drew, it meant he could come and go as he pleased, and not have to worry about hiding his face.

Paul, looked at his friend, who was concerned over Drew, "Phil, I have an idea! If, I can talk Gail into going back to the island, why can't you do the same with Drew?"

"Damn it Paul, why didn't I think of that!"

"Look,...I'll persuade Gail, while you persuade Pappy, to get back up into the sky. Tell him, it would do him some good to lay around for a few days and relax. Of course, you know where he goes for that!"

The two men looked at each other, and clasped hands, as Paul laughed saying, "Did you ever think we would end up playing cupid?!"

"Hell No!! ...I only hope we're doing the right thing."

Gail, left the hospital with a heavy heart, she really didn't want to take time off right now, but she had to get away from Drew. his bandages were to come off tomorrow, and he just couldn't see her,..not now.....when there was more surgery to be done. He, would be free to leave the hospital for a week or so, then return for the last operation that was scheduled.

Gail, wanted to say good-bye, but twice in a life time was just to much. She knew she wasn't that strong, instead, she took the cowards way out, by taking a leave of absense. As she was about to leave for the day, she could see Doctor Philip, coming towards her. "Gail! Wait please!" he called to her, stopping her in her tracks. He reached for her hand, pressing the key to the beach house into it, and told her to go there, that it would be good for her to get away from everyone, meaning his friend Pappy, and try to pull yourself together.

Later that night,Gail called her sister, to tell her that she was taking Philip's advice and was going back to the island. She didn't know how long she would stay, but she would give her a call when she returned. Hearing the concern in her sister's voice, she told her not to worry, that she was going to be fine. When she hung up the phone, she decided to pack, as she wanted to get an early start in the morning.

As she took her suit cases down once more, she began to think of Drew. Everything she packed reminded her of something that they had done. Like now, as she folded her halter top into the suit case. She could see herself, as she had walked so brazenly on the beach, with it partly opened, then taking it off all together. She blushed, as she remembered how she had removed her shorts, to stand nude before him. Even now, she could feel his eyes on her, as he had watched her that day so long ago.

Oh God, why can't I turn the clock back and start over with him? She asked herself over, and over again. Oh why…didn't he stay and give her a chance to prove her love for him, that his looks meant nothing to her, that loving him and having that love in return, was all that mattered.

As her tears fell into her clothes that she was packing, her mood changed. She suddenly got mad at herself. Why couldn't she be happy for him, and just stay out of his life? She was going to do everything in her power to forget him. Starting now! She looked down at the binoculars, that she held in her hand, and swore, "Damn it!" as she threw herself onto the bed, only to soak her pillow with tears once again.

As Bill, piloted the boat around, to bump gently along the side of the wharf, Gail, ran to the edge and grabbed the lines to tie it fast. Bill smilled, as he looked up at her saying, "You're getting to be a first class mate!" "Ya, next time I'll be the captain, and you can be the mate!" she hollered back, at this man, that was now laughing at her.

It took two trips, to carry all of Gail's luggage up the all fomiliar stair, that led to the beach house. Then Bill, carried in a small supply of fire wood, as the days and nights were getting chilly. "Please Bill, stay and have a cup of coffee with me before you leave?" "Just one, then I really have to leave, before the tide turns."

When Bill left, Gail ran out to the bluff and stood there waving until the boat disappeared from view. Feeling a chill in the air, Gail pulled her jacket closer around herself, as she headed back to the beach house.

Bill had started a fire, in the fire place, and now the room felt warm and cozy. First things first, she said to herself, as she made herself a drink and turned the radio on. As the music filled the room, it put her into motion, and she began to dance around the room. While still dancing, she picked up a box that was sitting on the floor, and never missing a step she started putting things here and there. Books went on the end table and her sun- tan lotion, in the medicine cabinet. When she opened the medicine cabinet, her mood changed, and she stopped dancing.....for there was the tube of salve that Drew, had rubbed so gently on her. Closing her eyes, she longed for the feel of his hands on her body. As she closed the cabinet, she got a glimpse of herself in the mirror. Her face was flushed from her thoughts, and her eyes were still puffy from crying half the night before. Turning quickly, she raced back into the living room, to turn off the radio. Then she carried her suit cases into her bedroom and began to unpack. Once this was done, she took a long hot bath, to relax hoping to get a good nights sleep. Stepping from the tub, she dried off, then wrapped a large bath towel around herself, and headed for her room. When she reached her bedroom, she stopped…then continued on down the hall until she was in front of the room where Drew, had slept.

As she entered the darkened room, she looked around through blurred eyes, remembering the last time she had been there. Moving closer to the bed, her heart began to beat faster, as she slowly pulled back the spread, and slipped between the sheets,letting the towel drop to the floor.

Tossing and turning, she remembered how wildly they had made love. Holding and caressing each other until they fell into an exausted sleep. She wished that she had met him sooner and under different circumstances. All she knew about Drew was that he had been in the service, and now owned and operated his own helicopter service. That he had a good mind and would make a loving husband, and a terrific father someday.......He needed so much love, that her heart ached knowing that she would never be the woman in his life. For he knew practically nothing about her.....except that she was the girl that had fallen in love with him on an island. Because of this great love for him she knew, she had lost him forever!

Hugging his pillow to her, she fell asleep with his name on her lips.

Three days had passed and High Pockets, was no where to be found. Today Drew's bandages were to come off and he wanted her there for good luck. He knew that he loved

Gail with all his heart....but this other woman had come to mean a great deal to him as a friend.

When Dr.Paul came in, Drew asked him where High Packets was. The Doc looked the other way as he didn't know what to say, then he quickly stated matter-of factly, "She's taking her vacation"

"But.....but she never said,Good-bye!" Drew cried out in anger and disappointment.

Soon the bandages were removed and he opened his eyes slowly as Doc held up a mirror for him to see his new face. Drew just held the mirror in his hand, never taking a look as he shook his head saying, "Damn it Doc, she never said she was leaving so soon!"

"Look Drew as a friend, take my advice and go to the island and heal yourself before your next operation. Maybe you'll find peace of mind there and you'll feel better than ever when you get back." In his heart Drew knew he couldn't go back to the island, without Gail, it would be torture.....He was hardly paying attention to Dr.Paul, as he kept on talking,"You know Philip will let you have the beach house for a couply of weeks. Think about it......it will be good for you."

Drew did think about it a lot. The bandages were off and the doctor's told him that the redness and swelling on his face would disappear.

Picking up his overnight bag he leaned into the mirror for one last look before leaving the hospital. He studied his face and had to agree with the doctors that after the last few scars over his eye were fixed, he wouldn't be bad looking. For the first time he could look at himself, with out cringing. He smiled at the reflection in the mirror as he put on a pair of dark glasses and saluted........and walked out!

Back at the apartment, Drew paced his room, longing for the comfort of Gail's arms. In his heart he knew thart she was the only woman he could ever love. As he looked out the window at the night sky, he spoke to the heavens saying, "I don't know where you are tonight Gail but I'm going back to the island and when I come back, I'll get my eye fixed up, then I'll find you! Wherever you are!......This I promise you.......and when I find you I'll never let you go!"

Drew no sooner hit the bed when he drifted off to sleep, only to dream of Gail calling to him.

During the night Drew rolled over and was suddenly wide awake. Reaching over he turned on the light, as he sat up running his hand threw his hair and swearing, all at the same time, "God damn it!.......I have to get out of here! I can't take another night of tossing and turning. I need some sleep!"

As he looked at his watch he threw his legs over the side of the bed grumbling, "Christ, it's three-thirty in the morning. If I leave now, I can be on the island by four-thirty." Having made up his mind he threw a pair of pants and a couple of sweaters, along with a few necessary things he would need for a few days in a duffel bag. Then grabbing his keys to the helicopter, he headed out of his apartment. When he reached the street, he hailed a cab and told the cab driver where to take him and to ...." step on it!"

Once in the air Drew relaxed and settled down. He smiled, as he looked at the picture that was pasted inside the cockpit. It was of himself and his buddy, Al. They had a sure thing going for them. He promised himself, that when he returned he would tell Al, that his idea for expanding the company was a good one, and to go ahead with it.

Looking down he could see the outline of the island and the white of the waves braking over the rocks below. He maneuvered the helicopter and sat it down on the far side of the island, as he had done many times before.

Grabbing his bag and a flashlight, he made his way to the backdoor of the beach house where he let himself in. He headed straight for his room knowing that he'd have no problem sleeping now.

As he entered the bedroom he didn't bother to put on a light, as he had been use to walking around in the dark for some time now. He slipped off his shoes and socks and as he crossed the room he discarded his clothes, starting with his sweater, and ending with his underwear, which he kicked onto a chair, as he passed it.

Placing his watch on the bed stand he lifted the covers and slipped into bed. he yawned and rolled over onto his side, closing his eyes.'God,' he thought,' the bed feels good.' The last thing he remembered was the sound of the waves hitting the beach.

Sometime later, Gail rolled over in her sleep and curled against something warm and smooth, only to be pulled closer to the heat, by a pair of strong arms.

Opening her eyes Gail realized that someone was in bed beside her. She screamed, as she rolled off the bed taking the bed spread with her! The light beside the bed clicked on as Drew, yelled, "You!"

"Oh my God, Drew!" she was bearly able to answer, in a relieved voice. Pulling the bed spread around herself she asked, "Where did you come from? How long have you been here?"

Drew was speechless, as he took her in from head to toe, for he knew he had never seen her as beautiful as she was to him at this moment. "Gail, Ahhhhh Darling, I didn't know anyone else was here....let alone you!" as he reached across the bed to her the sheet dropped exposing his nudity, as well as his desire for her. Gail never knew who touched the other one first, for all she saw was the man that she loved more than life itself reaching out to her.

"Darling," she cried, as she dropped the bedspread and went in to his arms. He held her close both of them kneeling on the middle of the bed as she broke down and cried. Drawing her closer in his arms he whispered the words that she had been longing to hear. "Oh Gail Darlin, I never thought I would ever hold you like this again." As he talked, he kissed her hair, her eyes,her mouth than buried his face into her neck, until her sobs subsided

Then he edged her down onto the bed, so they were facing each other, as he looked at her through misty eyes, he whispered, "I thought that I was was dreaming when I saw you standing there. It was like all my prayer's had been answered."

While he talked, Gail kept running her hands threw his hair then onto his shoulder and on down over his hairy broad chest, that heaved to her touch.

For by touching him was the only way she knew for sure that she wasn't dreaming. "Ohhh....I love you so much," she confessed, between burning kisses. "I've missed you so and I need to feel your arms around me." Then ....just a touch of panic crept into her voice, as she pleaded, "promise me you'll never leave me again? No matter what!.....Promise me!"

"Ahhh Darling, I'll never leave you again.........a day never went by but I thought of you,longed for you," he whispered against her trembling lips,

"I love you......love you.....love you." As he poured out his love for her, he drew her closer to the length of his body, that was now burning out of control with desire. For he had never wanted to be inside of a woman as he was at this moment.

As he felt himself hardening, he groaned as he kissed her passionately

Her lips parted, and his tongue played little darting games, in and out of her warm and inviting mouth, until her passion matched his. She sighed, as she drank in the taste and feel of his warm and demanding body. With his lips never leaving her's,he ran his hand down over her breast only to stop and tease each hardened tip with ecstasy. His hand traveled down over her slender hips, to feel and hold her bottom, which he pulled in closer to his enhanced manhood.

All the while Gail gave him back kiss for kiss as she trailed her hands over his muscular arms that held her so close, then sliding her hand over his shoulder and down to his chest where she ran her fingers thru his curly hair where she teased each flat nipple, as he had done to her until, she heard him utter a groan from deep in his throat. He pulled back giving her excess to the pulsing joy, that was waiting for her touch. As she slipped her hand down over his tight muscular stomach to the curly hair that led the way, she deepened her kiss, as her hand came in contact with his swollen member.

Feeling her hands on him he quickly passed his hand up the inside of her thighs where her moist warm center was waiting for the delight that only he knew how to kindle. As they moved with each other, Drew took his lips away from her's to slide them down her throat, and on to the valley between her breasts. There he lingered to taste and to tease each bud between his teeth, until he heard her moan as she called out his name, as she drew and held his head closer to her breasts.

As he lowered himself to her, she called out his name as the feel of his naked body resting on her's sent out shivers that she was unable to control.

Not being able to stand it any longer, she called out his name passionately'

"Drew....Oh Drew" ......Hearing this, he lifted himself up and positioned himself between her legs, She turned her head and kissed his shoulder wildly as he entered her. "Oh Drew.....yes....yesssssssss," she cried out as she automatically locked her legs around him, as if to never let him go. She arched up her back to meet each new thrust with a burning desire to take all of him. The room was silent except for the noises made by the motion of the bed, and the endearments that were whispered or called out in their mounting passion.

As their rhythm quickened with each stroke he took her to paradise with him. "Oh God Gail," he moaned through clinched teeth, as he spent himself inside of her.

Exhausted, they rolled over still clinging to each other, as she whispered, "I love you darling." He kissed her eyes and her swollen lips, that smiled up at him as he pulled the sheet half way up over them, then reached for the light and once again he was in darkness, only this time he had the girl of his dreams in his arms.

When he bent his head down to rest against her head, he felt a lump rise in his throat, as he realized that his face was never mentioned, and it really didn't matter to either of them, for this was true love.

Gail snuggled into his shoulder and sighed as the night and the sound of the surf lulled them to sleep, locked tight in each others arms.

When Drew opened his eyes, he looked at the sleeping woman that was snuggled up against him in slumber. He had so much to tell her about himself, and the fact that he wanted her to be in all of his future plans.

He felt that he was ready for anything that life would hand him. From now on, with Gail at his side....he could do anything! Gail looked so peaceful sleeping that he eased himself out of bed and headed for the shower. Once he had done this, he grabbed a pair of jeans and a tee-shirt putting them on as he headed for the kitchen.

Drew made coffee, then opened the refrigerator to hopefully find bacon and eggs. Just then he heard a noise and turned to see Gail standing there, as she came toward him smiling she asked, "Why didn't you wake me? Here, let me help you. Why don't you sit down and I'll make breakfast."

While she talked, he pulled her back into his arms and kissed the back of her neck, whispering, "you were great last night," and with a little chuckle he added, "want to go another round right now?" "Drew, stop it!" she laughed, "or I'll never get breakfast made."

He watched, as she walked around the kitchen and he knew that she had nothing on under her white satin robe. He could feel the need for her again and hoped that she was a fast eater....as things were beginning to rise beneath the table, and he didn't know how much longer he could control himself.

When Gail put down his plate in front of him, she tried not to get to close, as he would place his hand on her bottom and gently caress her. His touch telling her something, and she smiled at him, every time he made a grab for her, but she knew that they needed food to keep up their strength as she had plans of her own!

When she told him this, he just laughed saying, "Well then.....eat hearty, for I have plans for you Baby!?"

The days flew by all to fast. They were filled with walks on the beach and lying around under the sun. They couldn't seem to get enough of each other, for just one look in any direction would start their blood racing enough for them to be in each others embrace once again.

Taking Gail's arms from around his neck, Drew pushed her gently aside as he turned and sat up, pulling his cap down to shade his face, as a cold breeze came rushing off the water. "I think we had better get back to the house. The wind is getting just a little bit to cold." Standing up, he extended his hand to Gail, pulling her up against himself as he lowered his head and stole another kiss saying, with a grin on his face, "I'm hungry for food and you!"

"O.k. I'll make the salad, but....you get to do the steaks!" laughed Gail, for she knew better then to get near the stove. For he would be right behind her with his hands on her breasts. God....how she loved it when he did that, but the food never got cooked either! She giggled softly, when Drew asked," What's so funny?" "Oh... nothing,"answered Gail through laughing eyes.

"Oh Ya!" He yelled, as he made a grab for her. Turning she made a dash for the house. Laughing as he caught up to her, he playfully slapped her on her behind as she ran ahead of him.

Supper was perfect and so was the wine that they now sipped slowly. Holding the glass to her lips, she looked over the rim at Drew and murmured,

"I've never been so happy. I wish time could stand still right now....forever."

"I know darling, I never thought I would be able to look any woman in the eye ever again....let alone hold one in my arms, or love one as I love you." Reaching over, he took her hand in his and brought it to his lips, where he kissed it. Holding her hand between his, he looked deep into her eyes saying, "I'll always love you Gail, but... I have a couple more operations to get through before I can make any definite plans for the future. All I know is that I want and need you in my life. I need your love and the strength from that love, to see me through the hard times ahead." As he talked, Gail came around to sit on his lap, her arms going around his neck, where her finger-tips caressed the back of his neck, as she kissed him passionately, over and over again stirring their passion, that was like a flame waiting to be rekindled.

He kissed her back madly and while still kissing her he scooped her up into his arms and carried her into the front room, where he layed her gently on the rug. Lying down beside her, he kissed her again then bit her lower lip gently." Later Babe," he whispered, as he took her mouth once more before rolling off her. Then with a crazy smile that turned her inside out he asked,

"What do you say Babe, how about a little home made popcorn and a drink while we listen to the game?"

Knowing he would get his own way in the end, she got up with a sigh answering, "O.k. Pal!" As she disappeared into the kitchen where she leaned against the sink shaking and trying to calm herself down. Damn him! How can he turn it off and put it on the back burner for later! By the time the pop corn was ready, she was her old self again. She could hear the football game starting and she smiled as she headed toward the living room.

Drew could hear the pop corn popping, as he started to make them a drink. While making them he thought to himself, 'I better make these drinks strong, for we're going to need it when I tell her, that I have to leave tomorrow.'

As he thought of the surgery that he was going to have in two days, he broke out in a cold sweat. God, he thought to himself, 'I hope that High Pockets will be there with me. She's been like a pillar of strength. She has seen me at my worst. Thank God, Gail never saw me like that! I don't think I could stand it. He remembered the burning pain that made him cry out for help and the gentle hands that calmed him down, while a needle would be put in his arm to lessen the pain.' He was sitting with his eyes closed when Gail came into the room.

"I hope your not sleeping after I made all this pop corn!"

"Never happen," he said, as he patted the cushion beside him for her to sit down. They sat eating and drinking, while listening to the game. A silent peace had taken over as they sat side by side, with his arm around her.

Later as they lay in bed, he held her tightly in his arms as he told her how he had to leave the next day. As she started to protest, he told her it would only be for a little while, that she was to give him her telephone number and he would call her every chance he got.

"Please," she begged, "Let me come to the hospital and be with you!"

"No!" he answered in a stearn tone, as he sat up in bed. "I can't have you there. Can't you understand that?"

"No, I know you love me and that's enough to get me through. I just couldn't take it, if you were there when the going gets rough." He couldn't tell her how he had watched wife's and girl friends come to stay for hours at a time holding their man's hand through their pain. Only to turn and get out of sight of their loved one's and cry, for the agony they shared with them. No....this he didn't want for

Gail to ever go through! With Gail's love and High Pocket's reassurance…..he would make it.

All he could do now was to hold her and caress her until she became a moving passionate women beside him. Every nerve in his body came alive with the feel and the sent of her. Never, had he felt this way about any other woman…. never had he needed, or wanted any one as he wanted this woman that lay so plaintive in his arms. All he wanted was to be deep inside her, as if to become part of her, for he needed her tonight as never before.

Sensing his need, she pressed her body close to the length of his as her finger-tips moved slowly over his arms and shoulders, then to his broad chest. Looking up at him, he was consumed by the fire in her eyes, by the way her lips clung to his, by the intake of her breath as she sighed with delight, as she rotated her hips against him while reaching for his hardened member.

With a groan from deep within his throat, he forgot all about his surgery and the thought of leaving her the next day. "Ohhhhh Christ…Sweetheart…How good that feels……..Then he fell to caressing her until their bodies matched each others needs and desires.

He leaned over and kissed her waiting trembling lips, then on down to her breasts where her nipples were hard and swollen with anticipation of his mouth. As he licked and nibbled at her breasts, she twisted and moaned as she grabbed and held on to his bottom as she arched her body up to meet his. As his hand slipped down further, to where she was warm and moist, he dared not linger to longas he felt himself getting ready to explode. He then raised and positioned himself as he slipped into her. As he thrust with more ardency then before, she cried out his name, as he buried his face in her hair as they climaxed together.

Through deep ragged breaths he managed to whisper, "I love you......Love youuu..."

Sex was always good between them, thought Gail, but...tonight there was a closeness that she could not explain. They held each other close, cocked in each others arms as the still of the night took over. The sound of the surf hitting the shore was like their heart beats, Always together, beating in rhythm just as the ocean stayed in rhythm with each wave that broke over the shore.

The next morning as Drew looked into the bathroom, he could see Gail standing in the shower. He wanted to join her there just one more time but he noticed that her shoulders were shaking, and knowing that she didn't want him to see her crying he stepped back quietly, and went back to packing.

While Gail made breakfast, She noticed Drew'a duffel bags near the door. As tears sprang to her eyes, she said to herself,'no!...No more tears, he doesn't need this.'

After Drew had showered and dressed, he headed for the kitchen where Gail would be waiting with breakfast. He kept telling himself, 'keep away from her.....keep my hands to myself'.... for he knew if he even touched her once, he wouldn't be able to leave her. "I just want coffee," he said, as he reached for a mug from the shelf, "I never eat before flying." He was lying, and she knew it. Her eyes never left him, as she wandered around the kitchen. She really didn't know what she was doing. All she knew was that she had to keep busy, or she would throw herself into his arms and beg him to take her with him.

When Drew put down the empty mug and headed for the door, Gail took a letter from her pocket and handed it to him, telling him to read it later when he was alone and that her telephone number was in it, and for him to be sure to call. "Reverse the charges....I don't care," was all he heard as he started for the door.

"Please Drew, let me come to the helicopter with you!" Looking down into her misty eyes and knowing he needed to hold her just one more time,, he answered, "All right but it's not going to be easy for either of us."

After holding her in his arms and kissing her for what seamed be the hundredth time, he gently untangled her arms from around his neck and quickly got into the chopper without a backward glance.

Over his shoulder he jelled back, "See you in a few weeks and I'll call you! I love you Darling!'

AS the engine started up, he could see her calling to him that she loved him too, and throwing kisses as the propellers started turning, raising the sand only to block her out of his sight until he was high above her. Looking down at her, he knew he had found his mate at last that he loved this woman that was fading from sight. His looks and scars meant nothing to her, and because of this, he felt he could look anyone in the eye without turning away. He finally realized,that looks really didn't matter when you're really in love, for she had given him back his life, and all his dreams just by loving him.

As Gail watched him disappear from sight, she had a sick feeling in the pit of her stomache.......for she knew, that he expected to see High Pockets, ahd she didn't have the heart to tell him that it was her all along. He must never know!.... She suddenly felt fear creeping into her heart and she couldn't shake the feeling.

'I'll just atay on my ward and he'll never know I'm here.' As she thought this she had a sinking feeling that she had aready lost him. Feeling a cold chill settle over her, she turned and walked slowly back to the beach house, knowing that without him at her side, the last two days on the island would be tough.......

As Drew flew back to the helicopter service that he owned, he had a heavy heart. He could still see Gail in the shower, pushing her hair back as he had seen her do so often lately. He remembered how the soapy water gently caressed her body as it trailed down her shoulders and over her firm full breasts, then down over her flat stomach to rise over her hair covered mound, that brought him so much pleasure, then to trail down her legs, that had held him so close, only to make soapy swirls as it clung to her feet, before it disappeared.

Every inch of her was beautiful to him. There and then, he made up his mind that just as soon as his face was fixed up, he was going to marry her....and the sooner the better! With this thought in mind, he had a smile on his face as he touched down and was greeted by Al and Nancy.

Al shook his hand, while Nancy, got up enough nerve to kiss him for the first time. He hugged her saying, "I hope you two are ready to hold down the fort for the last time?"

"Oh Drew, you know we really run this place!" spoke up Nancy, as she grabbed his arm and headed for the office. It was a happy threesome that went back to work.

CHAPTER FOUR

When Drew regained consciousness, he called out to High Pockets, and was told by a soft voice, to try and sleep. As if on command he dozed off. When he awakened the next time, he was back in his room.

Drew knew the operation was over, when he felt the bandages on his face.'Thank God, it's over,' he thought to himself. He sensed some one was in the room, just as Paul said, "Ah...you're awake. Don't try to talk just yet. Every thing went well.....there will be a little discomfort for a day or so, but we'll give you something for the pain." Then as he felt for Drew's pulse, he asked, "are you in any pain right now?"

After answering "No." Drew asked," Is High Pockets here?" He needed to talk to her. He had so much to tell this nurse, for they had become good friends, and he wanted to tell her about Gail, and there plans for the future. Knowing, that she too was in love, made it all the better........she would be happy for him. For hadn't she said, "Maybe their life's would take a turn for the better."

Before Dr. Paul could answer him, a nurse came in and gave him a short. As Drew was drifting off, he heard her say, "He'll sleep through the night now."

On the way to work, all Gail could think about was Drew. Paul had told her, that he would call her down to the doctors lounge when the operation was all over. "Please God," she prayed, "let every thing be all right and Please Don't Let Him Find Out About Me!..............I love him and I can't loose him now."

All morning Gail's nerves were on end, her stomach felt like it was tied in knots and it was hard for her to keep her mind on her patients. Over and over in her mind she kept repeating, he'll be fine..... Paul was a wonderful surgeon, but it didn't help, as the time went by.

Later, a nurse came in to relieve her, telling her that she was wanted in the doctors lounge. Gail thanked her, and was on her way in no time!..She tried to walk as fast as she could without running, when she finally reached the doctors lounge, she was out of breath. As she opened the door, the look on Paul's face told her everything. He opened his arms to her and she ran into them. The tears she had been holding in all morning flowed freely now as Psul held her until she was able to speak. Looking up at him, she begged through happy tears, "Tell me everything."

Paul,told her how Drew asked for High Pockets, and how he didn't know what to tell him. HE also told her that Drew would be able to tell if he was lying to him....and he didn't want to break the confidence that Drew had for him. Paul walked away from Gail, then turned and looked at her, not as a brother-in-law, but as Drew's doctor. "Gail you know I have to be truthful with Drew, on all matters at this time. His health has to come first, above all else,....even your love for him."

Gail knew he was right, and as she wiped away her tears, she answered timidly, "I know Paul, do what ever you see fit......Drew must come first."

Gail went back to the ward knowing that Drew was all right, but saddened by the fact that she loved him, and could not be near him now, when he would need her the most, as High Pockets.

Gail didn't have time to think about Drew, as she had two new patients on her ward, and they needed all of her attention. She was glad when her shift was over, instead of staying later as she usually did, she headed for the exit, as if someone was after her. She wanted desperately to see Drew, just for a few moments, but she knew she couldn't take the chance of being recognized.

That night, she had a hard time falling asleep. She couldn't get Drew out of her mind. She only hoped and prayed that she was doing the right thing, by not telling him that she is High Pockets. Little did she know, the turn of events that would come from using a nickname.

Two days later, Dr.Paul, removed the bandages, then replaced them with smaller one's to enable Drew to open his eyes and see again. The stitches would be removed at a later date. Things were better than expected, and Drew was getting anxious to leave the hospital. Still, he was puzzled, it wasn't like High Pockets not to drop in.

The next day when Gail parked her car in the hospital parking lot, she sat there for a few minutes, trying to muster up her strength not to go in an see Drew. After taking a deep breath, she stepped out of her car, locking the door behind her, unaware that someone was watching from a third floor window.

Looking down, Drew watched as a pretty nurse got out of the Caramero, that he had admired a few weeks back. 'I might have known it would belong to a woman. only a girl would buy a candy apple red Camero!'

Smiling he turned and headed back to bed, just as a candy striper came in with his breakfast. She was a pretty little thing, and he tried to make her feel comfortable as he could, seeing that she was about to drop the tray and run!

"Hello, your new here arn't you?" he asked,with a smile. "Yes, today is my first day and i'm a little nervous.' she answered,with a smile.

Don't worry about it, you'll do just fine. Just keep that smile on your face and everyong will love you."

Feeling more at ease, she took a good look at his face, then smiled, saying," Thanks Mr. Hatfield, your all right!"

"By the way, call me Pappy, everyone else does."

"O.k, Pappy, see you at lunch." She was gone, as quick as she came in. Drew laughed, as it felt good to be able to talk to young people again, without having then turn away in disgust.

After he ate, he pushed back the tray and fixed the bed so he was comfortable, then laid back and closed his eyes. What seemed like a long nap was only a matter of minutes, when he was awakened by a nurse telling him to roll over, as it was time for his shot. "Boy....they named that right, when they said shot!...That's just what it felt like" The nurse was still smiling as the door closed behind her.

By late afternoon, Drew had asked everyone that had come in if they had seen High Pockets? No one seemed to know who she was. By four o'clock he dicided to take matters into his own hands...as he had felt an attraction to this woman every time she had been near him or their hands had come in contact with each other.

Just as he started to get out of bed, a nurse came in and asked him where he thought he was going? "Just for a walk down the hall," he lied.

"Oh No, Mr. Hatfield, not until your doctor gives his permission. Back to bed now, what you need is plenty of rest." after she smoothed the cóvers, she left the room, knowing that he was in bed where he belonged.

"You old bastard," he said aloud, as he rolled over and flicked the telivision on to watch the football game. Every thing had gone wrong, and he hoped the Patriots would at least beat the Miami Dolphins, to make up for it, not to mention the twenty bucks he had riding on the Patriots! While watching the game, he thought of Gail, and dicided to give her a call. Switching off the television, he picked up Gail's note and read it for the hundredth time.

Darling,
I'm thinking of you all the time, and I know that you're going to be fine. If anything goes wrong, please be-leave me when I say, I love you, and I know we can work things out. I love you desperately!
Call me 262-3300
Love Always
Gail

It was later that night, that Drew finally dialed Gail's number. The phone rang three times before a sleepy voice said, "Hello"

"Gail, it's me Darling."

"Oh Drew, I miss you so much. Are you all right? Are you in any pain?" She couldn't ask him enough questions, once she heard his voice.

"I'm fine sweetheart, and I'm not in any pain, except for the one's that the nurses make sure to give me, every three hours for infection. They just love my bottom for a target!" They both laughed and talked, until Gail told him that it was late and he needed his sleep.

Before he hung up, he told her how he had asked the nurses if they knew High Pockets, but no one seemed to know her.

"Drew, forget her, she probably left for a better job," she lied, as she began to panic.

"Ya, maybe your right Darlin."

"Drew, please hang up first, I hate saying good-bye."

"It's not good-bye Darlin, it's just goonight." as he threw her a kiss over the phone, he gently replaced the receiver back in it's cradle.

The night nurse came in and gave him a sleeping pill, telling him to sleep well. As he rolled over, his thoughts went to High Pockets. He fell asleep thinking of what he would do tomorrow, in order to find her.

On the other side of town, Gail drew the covers up around her shoulders and snuggled down, as she had a bad feeling of what tomorrow might bring.

Drew,could hardly wait until the nurse left the room, to make her morning rounds. While the nurses were busy bathing patients, he thought that this would be the ideal time to look for High Pockets, on his own!

As he slipped thru the corridors unnoticed, he held his breath. One more turn and he would be on the childrens ward, where he had heard High Pockets, taking care of children, only a few weeks ago.

Entering the ward, he stood looking around until he heard a voice telling a little girl that she was doing fine, and if she could lift her leg just one time, she would play a game with her. He watched in amazement, as the child who was badly burned, gritted her teeth, than raised her leg one more time. "Good Girl Virginia! I knew you could do it!"

Drew, knew there was no mistaking this nurse before him was High Pockets! Sensing someone was watching her, Gail turned around and looked up to see Drew standing there.

When she turned around, Drew thought he was seeing things. "Is that you Gail?" he asked, in a shocked voice, "you're High pockets!" He turned to leave, as he had seen enough to tell him that he had been tricked by this woman, as well as by his doctors. As fury raged within him, he new he had to get out of the ward....and fast!!

"Drew, please let me explain, it's all been a crazy mix up from the start!" she pleaded.

Drew turned to face her, his face white as ash, as he confronted her, "Drop the act Gail. You and the doctors had it all fixed up between you! What was it? Give the chump some hope and a couple of rolls in the hay, and the surgery would go on as planned! His eyes were blazing with anger, and his tone of voice told her that it was all over between them.

"Please Drew, I love you! Let me explain!" Tears sprang to her eyes, and her voice quivered as she pleaded again, "Don't go, please listen to me!"

"I've heard and seen all I want of both you and the doctors. I hope you all enjoyed yourselves at my expense. Just get the hell out of my life, and Stay Out!"

As he stomped back to his room, his eyes blurred, and he ran his hand over them, as if to clear them before anyone could see the tears that had slipped silently down his face.

Back in his room, he grabbed his over-night bag and quickly began to pack his things. As he took off his pajamas and robe, that Gail had given him, he ripped them in his haste to discard them, just as he had done to her

Picking up his bag, he turned to leave just as Dr. Paul came into the room.

"Pappy, don't be a fool! Stay and have the last operation. This is just a terible mix up! Please, it can be straightened out!"

"Get out of my way Doc......I don't want to hurt you,...but I will, if you don't move from the door......NOW!" he bellowed.

101

"Pappy, you've got stiches that have to be removed for God's sake, please don't leave like this!"

"Screw the stiches Doc! I'll find someone to take them out, and when I do….he won't be a lier like you!"

Paul knew it was fruitless to argue any longer, so he stepped aside. As Drew passed him, he gave him a look that Paul knew, he would never forget.

Once out of the hospital, Drew hailed a cab. All he wanted now was to hide from the rest of the world.

Being so up set, Gail ran crying out of the ward to the ladies room. She was heart broken, for she had destroyed the only man she could ever love. Not being able to get control of herself, she told the head nurse that she was leaving for the day. The children on the ward were quiet as mice, as they had never seen their Gail cry.

Gail's eyes stung, from pent up tears as she drove like a mad woman not caring about anything, just trying to get away from her pain and the pain that she knew she had caused Drew. Once inside her apartment, she thru herself across the bed and let out all her heartache. When her tears subsided, she fell into a restless sleep.

Later that night, Gail called her sister and asked her if she would get Drew's address and telephone number, as she had to speak to Drew. She couldn't let it end with him thinking that she had lied to him all this time, as a favor to Paul, and Philip.

Donna listened to the heartbreak in her sister's voice and she knew she had to help her. Gail, you know I'll do all I can for you. I'll talk to Paul, and I'll get back to you. Try not to worry…….things will turn out all right. I know it."
"Thanks sis, but I don't think I'll ever get him back ….but I have to explain things to him. I'll wait for your call."

As Gail replaced the phone in it's cradle, she knew that part of her life was over. At this moment, she just wanted to get away from the hospital,...and everything that reminded her of Drew. She couldn't cry, as she had no tears left to shed. For in a matter of minutes, she had become an empty shell of a woman.

That same afternoon, as Drew's taxi cab pulled up at the privately owned air strip, he was greeted by his partner AL, "Hi Drew! We didn't expect you back so soon." "Ya,...I had a change of plans and I had to get out of there in a hurry."

Sensing there was something, wrong Al just took his bag and followed him into the office, where he was greeted by Nancy. "Drew, you look tired, here...sit down while I get us all a cup of coffee."

Seeing the bandages still on his face, she asked, "Drew, arn't you out of the hospital alittle earlier than you should be?" Her voice was full of concern, as she watched him pacing around the office.

"Look," statedDrew, "so there will be no more questions after this, I was made a fool, of by my girl, who happened to turn out to be High Pockets, and my so called doctor friends! I'm not going to have the last operation because I don't give a damn about my face. I'll find a nother doctor to take out the stitches, but as far as I'm concerned.....I'm off women and doctors for life!"

"Drew, you must be mistaked, there must be a reason for all this. Didn't you talk to Gail, or the doctors?" asked Al, with concern in his voice.

"No! I didn't want to hear anymore of their lies. I don't want to discuss this ever again. That part of my life is dead and buried."

Nancy had to turn around as he talked, as her eyes filled with tears, for the heartache and despair she could sense in Drew's voice as he spoke.

Then to Nancy, he said, "I'm not in to anyone that calls from the hospital and you don't know were I am. Understand?"

"Yes Drew, I understand."

"O.k. now that that's taken care of, let's get down to business." stated Drew, and by the tone of his voice, the others knew he ment business. For the rest of the day, Al and Drew discussed and made plans for the enlarging the company. Drew was to get in touch with the bankers, while Al saw about a nother helicopter.

"Al, could I crash at your place for a couple of days,"asked Drew, """just until I figure out what I want to do?" "Sure, you didn't have to ask," then laughing he added," just bring your own beer!"

Both men smiled and shook hands. Not saying a nother word to each other they turned and went back to work.

Two weeks later, a red Camero pulled up in front of 'Pappy's Flight Service'. When Gail stepped out of her car, she looked around and saw two helicopters on the landing pad, and her heart began to play tricks on her, as she reconized the red and white. He must be here, she said to herself, as she drew in her breath and headed for the main door.

As she entered the small office, a pleasant woman in her fourties asked, if she could help her?

"Yes, I'd like to see Drew, if he's in."

"Whom shall I say is calling?"

"Tell him it's Gail."

Nancy's smile disappeared when she realized who this young woman was. Then she remembered Drew saying, that he was not in to her. "Oh...I'm sorry Gail, but Drew isn't in right now, and I don't expect him back today. Sorry."

"Please, I have to see him, It's important!"

"I'm sorry Miss, but it's impossible. Please leave." Nancy's tone of voice had changed, and Gail knew she was lying to her.

"All right," answered Gail in a huffy voice, as she was getting madder by the minute. "Would you please give him this?"

Feeling sorry for this young woman, that had caused her boss so much heartache, she finally said, "Yes, I'll give him a message."

Gail reached into her hand bag and took out a card, which she handed to Nancy. "Here, this is a number of a doctor that will remove Drew's stitches, and he is willing to perform the last operation."

"Please, I don'i know if Drew will want this," answered Nancy, with reproach.

"Please," begged Gail, "Give it to him and tell him I said, to stop pitying himself and to grow up, and to do this for himself!.......and as for women.......well he doesn't have to worry about them, because he'll be handsome when the stitches are out........and then he'll have women falling at his feet!"

Gail knew, Drew was behind one of the closed doors listening, but she couldn't stop talking once she got started, "and another thing, tell him that he wiped his feet on two good friends, Paul and Philip for nothing, and that a lot of people in this world are just as sick as he's been, only their scars are on the inside!"

As tears blinded her, she turned and ran to the door, only to push it, instead of pulling it open. Her tears over-flowed as she cried out,"Damn it!"

Then she pulled the door open and blindly ran to her car.

Nancy, sat there with her eyes covered, after she watched Gail leave in a cloud of dust.

Suddenly, the door opened behind her, as Drew walked in saying,"I'm sorry Nancy, that you had to hear all that. I should have faced her once and for all........God.......what a spitfire she is! I guess, that was one of the thingsI loved about her......she holds nothing back."

Just then Al came from the other office and quietly spoke to Drew, "Maybe you had better look up the doc's.........you could be way off base on this one. The little lady didn't sound like a liar to me, but a woman that's in love with a guy that's to blind to see it!"

'Please Drew,spoke up Nancy, in a calm voice, as she handed him the doctors card, "why don't you talk to Paul, and then if your not satisfied, look this doctor up."

Taking the card from her, he hesitated, then said, "I think I need to get up stairs for awile." He grabbed the keys to 'Number One' and stalked out of the office. As Drew was taking off, his two best friends watched from the window. Nancy wiped a tear away, as Al put his arm around her. "Maybe he'll think things over and then he'll do the right thing." whispered Al, as he gave her shoulder a little squeeze.

"I hope so, they love each other, I can tell....and now there hurting each other for no reason." answered Nancy, as she started to answer the telephone that was ringing off the hook!"

Two weeks later, as Drew flew thru the clouds, he kept hearing Gail say," Other people have scars, but they don't show." What did she mean by that? He thought about all that had happened, and he knew he needed some answers. Why had all of this happened? He knew he still loved her, no matter what he had said to her......but she had lied to him.....why?!....That's what he had to know, and he had to know now!!

Drew, turned the chopper around, and headed for the hospital. Twenty minutes later, he was landing on the pad. He knew it wasn't going to be easy, as he headed for the door and Dr.Paul's office.

The head nurse on the floor, paged Paul for Drew, then he asked, if she would please page Dr. Philip Fresno for him. He was told to go to the conference room, and they would be right with him.

While Drew waited, he paced back and forth, while a million questions came to mind. What was Gail doing on the island in the first place? Damn it! Why did she call herself High Pockets, only to me!? And why, hadn't she told him that she knew he was Pappy, when they met back at the island the second time? Suddenly, fear crept into his heart, as he remembered Paul saying, "I send patients and friends who need help, to my place, to relax." He could understand why he was sent there.....but why Gail?

Suddenly the door opened, and in walked two of his best friends. When they saw the misery in Drew's eyes, they held out their hands, only to have them clasped tightly by Drew. "Look guy's," Drew stammered, "I acted like a total ass, and I want to apologize to you both."

"Look Drew, all we want to do is to help you get back to your old self. You're almost there, so please let us help you. Give us two more weeks of your time and you can start a new life for yourself!" proclaimed Paul.

107

Drew looked at these two men, that had done so much for him and realized that they were looking out for his welfare. Then, with a smile spreading across his face, Drew finally agreed with them, "O.k. We'll continue with the plans for the operation. These stitches are itchy any way......I guess there pretty over due in coming out."

"Fine," spoke up Philip, before he could change his mind, "come on in to the next room and we'll remove them."

Ten minutes later in the examining room, Drew looked at himself after the stitches were taken out. "Not bad!" he smiled, for the first time.

Paul looked at him saying, "We only have to fix the corner of your eye where it sags, then we'll put a patch on it for a week, and then you'll be good as new."

"How about the day after tomorrow? If you clock in by six, you'll br awake by lunch." Promised, Philip.

"Great, I'll be there," answered Drew, as he stood up and ran his hand thru his hair saying, "Please guys, sit down, I have a few questions that have to be answered, I want the truth.....no matter who it hurts. Do I make myself clear?" The two doctors looked at each other and nodded yes. Paul knew it was time to tell the whole story.

"First, I want to know why Gail was on the island?"

Paul looked at him for a moment, then started to talk, "A few weeks before you met Gail, she had gotten emotionally involved with one of her patients, ... A five year old boy, who died in her arms, while she was rocking him......I guess it really started long before that. Gail had been a Navy nurse and had seen altogether too much death, and and pain, along with some terrible burn cases. When she was discharged from the Navy, she came here to the burn center, where she was needed. That she was!...God...she was heaven sent. Why, she could make people do things that they thought were impossible……..and they did it!! She would never let them give up.

Drew listened, taking everything in that Paul was saying. Then he asked, "Did she ever tell you that she had been a Navy nurse?"

"No….we never talked about her past or what she did for a living. It just never came up," replied Drew, as if in a daze." Well, Gail was loosing weight and crying all the time when no one was around,…..then she began staying later and later after her shift. She was heading for a nervous breakdown, and we didn't want to see that happen. So…..the two of us, got our colleague to examine her, and to tell her she had to take time off."

Philip interrupted, saying, "We decided to send her to the island. We didn't know that you would be there too! When Gail returned home, instead of a relaxed woman, we found a woman who had fallen in love with a man, who had left her,……for what he called, 'personal reasons of his own.' Even then,………we didn't put two and two together…..that it was you!"

Paul paced back and forth, as Philip talked, then came to stand in front of Drew. Looking down at his friend, he continued to talking, "Gail was over the house one night, and she had just come from visiting with you,……I think she had just bought you a pair of pajamas…..am I right?"

"Ya…she did Paul," answered Drew, with intrest creeping into his voice.

"Well, while she was crying on Donna's shoulder, she told her how she had seen your face, thru her binoculars, the day before you left the island.

She didn't give a damn what you looked like! Only now……..she knew why you were hiding in the dark all the time. Gail, figured you wanted to finish your surgery, and then, if you felt the same, you would find her. Don't you see! It had to be you doing the finding, or you would never believe she didn't love you out of pity. So......she let you fly away! Donna and I realized that night, that you were the man on the island. Gail, never knew you were at the hospital."

"Why didn't you both tell me then!?" demanded Drew, as he clinched his hands into fists, only to open them and rub his thighs, as he looked at them for as answer."

"Because your attitude had changed, and we wanted you to stay in good spirits until after your surgery. We knew, you needed a friend to help you thru the hard times, and who would be better than Gail," pointed out,Philip.

"Drew," said Paul, "I asked Gail, as a favor to me, to look in on a friend of mine that needed someone to talk to. As you were unable to see, or speak to her, you would never know who she was. That part worked.....We, just told her that you liked being called by you nick name, Pappy,......and so.......we suggested that she use her's, High Pockets. The boys in the service called her that. So......all the time she spent with you, she didn't realize it was you that she was taking care of. We both knew that when the bandages came off, she would know it was you. So....we had her take notes that day. Remember?"

"Ya Doc, I remember," as Drew spoke, he could still remember all that had taken place that morning.

"Well, when Gail saw your name, on the charts for the first time, she made a funny sound. Do you remember asking her if there was something wrong with your face?" And her answering. "No, I always cry when I'm happy."

"Yes I remember that," this time there was a lump in his throat, and he could hardly spesk.

"Gail, decided to go back to the island for a few days, so you wouldn't find out that she was High Pockets. But......Damn it to hell Drew, you had to drop in on her again!"

"I don't know what went on between you two, but it must have been terrific because Gail was radiant, when she came back home. When I asked her what she was going to do about you, she just laughed and said, "I'll stay on the ward and he won't even know I'm here. He's looking for High Pockets, not me!" She also said, that when your surgery was over, if by any chance you still wanted her, she would quit the hospital and become Mrs. Hatfield in a minute!" Paul looked down at Drew, "I'm sorry as hell about all that has happened, she loves you so much, that I'm afraid of what this will do to her."

When Drew looked up, the doctors knew he was beginning to put the pieces together. They just listened as he spoke, "You see Doc, I had one of the candy stripers take me down to the children's ward, before the bandages were taken off, the first time, so.....when High Pockets didn't come to see me, I decided to go to her. I wanted to tell her about Gail and I for I knew she would be happy for us. Because she had told me about someone she had loved and lost. God in heaven!! I nearly died. when I saw it was Gail all along! I guess I went a little crazy. All I thought, was that someone had played a trick on me, and I wasn't going for it......you both know the rest...I was a complete bastard to the one person I love, and rotten to the two best doctors in the world, that made my face over." At this point, he could endure no more, then as an uncontrollable sob broke from his lips, he covered his face with his hands, and cried openly for the first time.

"It's all right Drew,....... let it all out, you've been holding that in for a long time," said Paul, as he griped his shoulder real hard, with understanding and compassion.

At last, Drew understood why he felt so close to High Pockets, she and Gail, were one in the same person..........to love one was to love the other. When Drew finally got control of himself, he asked to speak to Gail.

The two doctors looked at each other and sighed.

"What's wrong now? Tell me," Pleaded Drew, as he stood up to confront them both, "Well?"

"She's not here any longer. She quit, two days after you left the hospital." stated Philip. "O.k! so she quit. Where does she live? I'll go there."

"You can't Drew," answered Paul, as he sank into a chair and ran his hand over his face," she packed a few bags and left the next morning for parts unknown. Donna, is going crazy, she's afraid something will happen to her."

"Didn't she say where she was going?" asked Drew with alarm.

"No, she told Donna, that when she decided what she was going to do, she would write. God.....Where would she go!?" Drew could hear the fear and concern in his voice, as he spoke of his sister-in -law.

"Paul, I have to find her! I love her and I can't loose her now. I 've been a stupid blind fool all to long. When I think of what I've put her through, I can't stand it, It's tearing me apart! We have to find her."

"Look Drew, have your surgery, and I'm sure within a couple of days we'll hear from Gail. Then you can go to her. It's for the best, please Drew, take our advice." pleaded Paul.

"Paul's right Drew, we'll all get on it and see what we can find out for you. Meanwhile....you get yourself in here and we'll have you fixed up in no time. Remember this.......she's done all this, just so you could have a chance at live as a normal person. Don't disappoint her now! "argued Philip.

Drew agreed, then shook hands with his friends and left.

Once back up in the clouds, his thoughts went to Gail "Oh Darlin, where are you? I have to find you, so I can tell you how much you mean to me. I love you and I'll never let ouy out of my life ever again." This he promised to himself.

He now realized how she had been sick herself, and had never mentioned it. Everything she had ever done was just for him. His heart ached, as he remembered all the terrible things he had said to her. "God" he promised, "If she'll have me after this, I'll make it up to her for the rest of my life."

All he could think of was, how she had done everything to help him, and he had hurt her so many times. He had never known a woman like her before. He had, had his share of woman before the accident, but.......he couldn't think of one of them, that had ever given anything to him,........they had always taken. Now, for the first time, he had someone that really cared for him.........and him alone. He knew, he had to find her soon, and he hoped and prayed that when he did, she would still love him. As he headed in for a landing, he knew just what he had to do!

Gail was still crying as she turned onto the highway. Having no particular place in mind, she just drove until it got dark. She pulled off the highway into a little town, and began to look for a place to spend the night. When she spotted the Holiday Inn, she turned in with a sigh of relief.

"Once in her room, she kicked off her shoes, and threw herself across the bed. Within minutes she was sound asleep. She was suddenly awakened by people laughing in the hallway. Reaching over, she picked up the phone and ordered a sandwich and a bottle of wine, to be brought to her room. Then she quickly undressed and took a quick shower. As she was slipping into her robe, there was a knock on the door." going to the door she asked, "Who is it?"

"Room service mam."

Gail opened the door, and the bell- boy placed the tray on the small table, then left after he received his tip.

Gail hadn't realized just how hungry she was until she began to eat. The wine was chilled and delicious, and she hoped it would help her to relax.

While she ate, her thoughts went back to that morning in Drew's office. She felt badly at how she had spoken to Nancy, who seemed like a nice person. "Damn you Drew! I hope that you get so mad at what I said, that you'll go to Paul, and have the last operation, just for spite! "Well…It was one way of making him do it ….if her plan worked.

She knew in her heart, that it was all over between them. Drew, would put his life back together and forget all about her. She had to find a way to get him out of her heart, then just maybe……she could get him out of her life,

Gail, knew more about his private life now, that she had lost him. She knew he was a helicopter pilot, but she never dreamed of him owning his own company, and that he lived just a few miles out of the city. Maybe things would have been different. if thay had known more about each other. But….they didn't, and now it's too late! As hot tears sprang to her eyes, she rolled over and burying her face into the pillow, as she cried for the one person that she loved most in this world.

CHAPTER FIVE

Gail rolled over to see the sun shinning in on her. As she strectched, she decided to shower and dress, then to get in her car and just drive anywhere........

For the first time it felt damn good not to have to look at the clock and hurry to work, Good....just to do as she damn well pleased! Gail was dressed in a pair of jeans and a warm sweater, as it was late October, and there was a chill in the air. She left out her wind breaker, for when she wasn't in the car. She had driven about ten miles, when she saw a dinner called, MOM'S & POP'S,, it seemed to beckon to her. After she had finished her pancakes and coffee, she felt much better. She, even smiled at a stranger in the next booth, and that was something she hadn't done in a long while.

Gail hadn't realized it, but as she rode along the highway she got nearer and nearer to the ocean. Soon she could see the water below her. and she pulled of the road onto the soft shoulder. She stepped out of her car, and leaned against the guard rail, as she watched the waves crashing over the rocks below.

Her thoughts went back to the island, then she remembered Philip saying, "No one ever goes there in the cold weather, especially in the winter." As if a light went on in her head, she hurried back to her car, and headed for the nearest telephone booth!

"Please Philip, be there," she prayed, as she dialed his number.

"Hello, Dr. Fresno, speaking."

"Hello Philip, This is Gail."

"Gail, where are you? We've all been worried sick about you."

"I don't know why.......I'm a big girl now. Philip, I have a proposition for you. I want to rent your house on the island, for three months. I know, no one has ever gone there in the winter,..... but I need to be alone, and this would be perfect for me! Please Phil, you haven't rented it to anyone, have you?" she asked, with great exportation.

"No I haven't, but Gail, when it gets real cold, you'de have to keep the fireplaces going. It's a lot of hard work chopping wood, and the winter storms will frighten you to death. I really don't know what to say Gail."

Hoping, he had discouraged her.

"No they won't, please Philip, I can have Bill take over supplies and extra fire wood during the month, and I'll manage just fine. Please,... say yes!"?" She knew, she was begging, but she didn't care.

"All right Gail, but just until January thirtieth. Then your to come home. Is it a deal?"

"Yes! Thanks Philip, you don't know what this means to me. You can tell Paul my plans, but no one else. I just want to get control of my life again. Remember.......NO ONE! Oh! How much is the rent?"

"For you," he chuckled, "Five bills a month. Is that too much?"

"No, it's wonderful. I'll send you a check for the full amount tomorrow. Will you tell, Bill, I'll meet him at the dock, the day after tomorrow, at ten in the morning?"

"Sure I'll tell him. Take care of yourself Gail.....bye."

"Bye Philip, and thanks." As she hung up the receiver, she smiled, as she had a feeling that she was finally going home. She, had to get back to where she had been the happiest,.... then..... maybe she could start her life over again,

She was almost happy, as she turned her car around and headed back to her apartment to pack.!

The surgery was over, and the doctors were pleased at the results, as they watched Drew, being wheeled out of the operating room.

When Drew awakened, he opened his good eye and could see a nurse standing near his bed. Seeing Pappy stir, the nurse asked, "How are you feeling? Would you like a drink?"

"Ya," he answered, trying to smile, and feeling a little bit woozy yet."

"Here you are," she said, as she held the glass for him. "The doctor will be in soon, try and rest, and I'll see about supper tonight."

"No don't, I won't be here for supper!"

"Oh NO!....Well, we'll see about that," she fumed, as she left the room.

"Damn old bitch, she'll never learn!" He couldn't help but laugh, for the last time he told the same nurse that.....he did leave!

Two days later, Drew started to look for Gail. Both he and Al, went over the highways and hotel parking lots in their choppers looking for Gail's red Camero. It was getting dark when they dicided to head for home. It was as if the earth had opened up and swallowed Gail's car. Drew knew it had to be either in a garage, or she had left town. Even though, Paul, kept telling him that Gail wasn't home, Drew kept ringing her number. Her phone rang and rang, but no answer. Swearing, Drew put down the receiver. Then getting out of his chair, he went to stand at the window, where he could look out over the city......Looking out into the darkness of the night, he vowed, "I know you're out

117

there darling, and I won't give up until I find you. No matter how far away you go, I'll find you! This I promise!"

While on the other side of the city, Gail was busy packing, when the phone rang for the tenth time. "Give it up!" she yelled at the phone. It had to be Donna, or the hospital calling, but she didn't want any one or anything to stop her from getting away.

Gail packed all of her old clothes that were warm, along with her boots and gloves, for when it would snow. Also, warm pajamas and her robe, these she knew she'de need. She packed books, magazines and a few tapes, as well as a couple of decks of cards, into a box, now..... she was all set to go!

After she had placed these items in the trunk of her car, she headed for the grocery store, where she made quick work of shopping. A teenage boy, helped her out to her car, and he laughed, when he saw all the stuff packed in her trunk.

"Boy! You must be going on one hell of a trip lady!"

"Yep, I'm doing just that."

After tipping him, he stood waving to her, as she pulled out of the parking lot. Now to the liquor store and then to the dock, where Bill, would be waiting for her.

When Gail drove up to the dock, she could see Bill putting things on the boat. She,started honking her horn, until he looked up and waved back at her. Suddenly, for the first time in years, she felt light hearted. She, was actually excited about going to the island.

Bill and Gail, hurried putting things on board, as Bill, often said

"You have to watch the tide."

"Bill, what about my car?" "I'll put a tarp over it for you. That will keep the weather off of it. Leave me your keys, and I'll try to find a garage for it before winter." "Thanks Bill, your're a love."

Bill thought to himself, this can't be the same girl? She made him laugh and feel good all over. He liked her, and he'd help her all he could.

Gail, I'll come by once a week until the middle of November, with fire wood, and supplies, then after that....your on your own. Remember, you can always call the Coast Guard in case of an emergency, and they would have you off this island in no time." He gave her a long serious look, then she reached up and kissed him on his cheek, saying seriously, "I won't forget."

Later that day, as they reached the island, Bill and Gail, worked side by side, as they carried all of her belongings up to the house. After everything was put safely on the porch, Bill, turned to say good-bye. He reached out and grabbed her, holding her tightly for a minute, then he was gone.

As the boat faded into the horizon, Gail worked fast, as she wanted to get all her supplies inside the house. Once this was done, she felt better. Taking of her coat, she started a fire in the fireplace in the living room and one in her bed room, as the house felt cool and damp.

While she put the groceries away, she made a hamburger for herself. This, with a few pickles and a Pepsi, would do nicely.

Later that night, as she sat curled up in her bathrobe, staring into the fire and listening to the music, that softly filled the room, her thoughts went to Drew.

She knew that by now, if he had decided to have the operation, that it would be over. Knowing the doctors, she knew, he would be in good hands, no matter who did the operation. She only hoped that he would pick up his life, and find happiness.

It seemed to her, that her life was like a roller coaster,....one minute she was loved, and happier than she ever hoped for,....then suddenly, she would be dropped, only to feel dead inside.

Twice, Drew had left her, and she knew she couldn't take a another rejection, like the last one. She was tired of making excuses for other people's actions. It was about time someone thought about her fears and needs. She had always given all of herself to her patients, and she was tired of being the one always to bend. Hugging her knees tightly to her chest, as hot tears threatened to fall, she made a promise to herself.....I'm going to start a new life for myself, and I won't let anyone or anything hurt me ever again. They say, "physician heal thyself" Well....this time I will!!

She knew in her heart, that it would be hard to forget Drew. As every where she looked, she could see him. His presents, was here in this room with her now,....Oh God,.....how was she ever going to forget him? She could still hear him saying, "Get the hell out of my life and stay out!" Oh God, she thought, he doesn't love me any more, he said that he didn't need me, and he never wanted to see me again,....I'll keep telling myself, he doesn't love me until I believe It! Suddenly she felt real tired, as she leaned her head back against the couch, with her eyes closed, listening to the surf hitting the beach. The never ending rhythm of the tide, willed her body to relax, and sleep finally took over.

Each day, Gail got up feeling better physically and mentally. She would start the day with a hot shower, and a big breakfast. Then she would take the hatchet, that she had found in the shed out back, and go to the futherest end of the island, to gather wood for the fire places. This was her main concern. Each day she would work closer to the house. As she walked, she picked up drift wood that she would pile up, every so often, along with small branches that she could hack off trees. She made a couple of trips a day hauling the wood in a box, that she had tied a rope to. It was almost like pulling a sled.

When Gail, reached the house for the second time, she was hot and sweaty. After she stacked the wood for the day, she got herself a glass of juice and went out back to sit on the porch to cool off. The exercise was good for her, and just being out doors and not having to watch the clock every minute, was begining to change her physically. She had been out all day with out a sweater on, and as she looked at her bare arms, she could see how tanned she had gotten.

The tide was going out when she finally went into the house to put on a sweater and a windbreaker on. As she went out the back door, she grabbed a bucket that was hanging on a nail, and headed for the beach,......swinging the bucket like a child, without a care in the world.

There, she knelt down and began to dig with her hands where little tiny bubbles appeared in the smooth sand. She, squealed with delight, as she turned over the small white clams! What a feed I'll have tonight, she thought to herself, and when it gets colder, I'll shuck and freeze them for chowder.

Later, as she sat eating the tasty clams, and thinking of all these she could eat while she was there. Knowing this, she could save the meat that Bill brought for the winter.

As she sat watching the sun going down over the water, a feeling of peace came over her, and she knew she was going to be all right. Yes......she had done the right thing coming to the island.

When Drew, had called it his," Island of Dreams,"……..little did he know…..that all she would ever have ……were………"Just Dreams."

Drew had, had the patch removed from his eye for a week now, and he had to admit, that he looked great. He had to get use to his new looks, as well as having people looking at him and not turning their eyes away, especially the younger generation. For they were bold with their remarks, like…"What a hunk! or Great buns!" Drew would just laugh it off, as it felt good to be a hole person again. He knew, he would never look the same as he did before the accident, but he could look himself in the mirror and not wish he were dead. He had a new face, and now he was going to start a new life.

Drew, took the steps two at a time, that led to Dr. Paul's front door. He was determined to find out where Gail was. He had taken enough bull, and now he wanted some straight answers!

Donna, answered the door and was surprised to see Drew standing there. "Drew, Come in. How well you look, and so handsome too! To bad I'm married," she laughed, as she reached up to kiss him in the cheek, for the first time. He kissed her back, then asked if Paul was in?

"Yes he is, go into the front room and I'll get him for you." She then turned, leaving him alone, as she quickly went to fetch Paul.

When Paul, came into the room Drew stood up and the two men shook hands," Hello Drew, I was expecting you to drop in, what can I do for you?" As if he didn't know. "Paul, do you know where Gail is? Please…..I have to talk to her."

"Drew, I won't lie to you. Yes, we know where she is, but we can't tell you. Gail, made us promise not to tell anyone. She needs to be alone right now, and decide what she wants to do with her life. I don't even know if she'll ever return to nursing. All I can say...is if you really love my sister-in-law, then give her some time.......and then find her."

Drew, sat down and buried his head in his hands, then he looked up at Paul, "I've looked every where, I've even gone up in the chopper and looked for a red Camero. I'll find her if it takes me a life time! I love Gail, and I've hurt her, but if I ever find her again, I'm going to marry her, before she can ever run away from me again." Just then, Donna came into the room carring a tray. "Come on guys, let's have some coffee and cake while we talk."

While they huddled around the coffee table, Donna, couldn't keep her eyes off Drew's face, as there was a sadness in his eyes that couldn't be denied. She wanted desperately to tell him where her sister was, because she knew that they loved each other. Her sister had proven it by letting him go. Now.....here he was sitting beside her, begging to know where she was. This she promised herself,....If he doesn't find her in two weeks,....... I'll tell him myself! No matter what Paul promised her sister.....

When Drew got up to leave, he looked at Paul, and asked, "Tell me one thing, is she all right? If she's ill, I want to know it now?!"

"No Drew, answered Paul," she's going to be physically fine, once she calms down. She's at a place that she loves. Try not to worry." Then he added with a smile, "but find her soon!"

When they closed the door behind Drew, Paul pulled Donna into his arms and held her close, "I know that was rough on you, but your sister needs a little space right now. If Drew, digs around in the right places, he'll find her."

Donna kept thinking to herself, 'Drew, think about the island!'

With their arms around each other, they headed for the stairs. All the lights were out and neither of them talked until they were ready for bed. Then Donna, broke the silence, "God Paul,... I wonder what Gail's doing now?" Seeing tears spring to her eyes, he embraced her, kissing her neck, as he whispered, "She's probably sound asleep. Just like we'll be later."

He laughed, as he pulled her gently down on the bed with him, only to love and fondle her, as he did so often. Paul knew, that all of his dreams were right in this woman that he loved so dearly.

"Paul don't," she murmured, but he only laughed back at her, as she was really saying, yes with her body! He pulled her close, as he tucked her beneath himself as he was about to show her just how much he needed her.

Then just before he made them one, he whispered, "Donna, don't ever leave me!"

"No Darling..........Never!"

It was the end of October, and the wind was blowing up a storm, as Drew decided he had better hit the grocerg store, or he was certainly going to starve! While he was pushing the shopping cart around, it hit him! Maybe Gail, had stopped here before she left town. Every one takes food on a trip, even if it's just a snack! Drew began to ask all the cashiers, if they had seen Gail, but no one seemed to know who he was talking about. Then he remembered the stock boys, they would remember a pretty face and a red Camero! He, had asked, four stock boys and they all had the same answer,..

"No." Just as he was starting to leave the store, he noticed a stock boy helping a woman, by putting her groceries into her car. He pushed his cart out the door, and called to the boy. "Hey Kid! Hey You!"

The stock boy looked up and started toward Drew, asking, "Did you want me mister?"

"Ya, about three weeks ago, a friend of mine left town and I wondered if you saw her. Her hair, is the color of honey, and she's about five foot five, and terrific looking. She drives a candy apple red Camero. Do you remember seeing her?"

Drew, held his breath as the boy thought for a moment, then his face broke out in a smile, as he remembered the terrific looking chick, and her dynomite car. "YA! She's a good looker! She gave me a big tip. Her car was loaded with everything!" The stock boy was laughing just thinking about all the junk a woman could fit in her car. Drew, laughed with him, as it was the first good lead he had.

"Tell me, what did she have inside her car, besides groceries?" inquired Drew, hoping the kid would remember.

"Mister….you name it, she had it! winter clothes mostly. Oh ya, a fishing pole and a box of tapes and books….and stuff like that. I asked her if she was going away for a year, and she just laughed and said, "No just," then he thought for a second, then said, "I think," she said, "Three months….she sure was nice."

"Thanks Kid, what's your name?"

"Tommy." As Drew, placed a twenty dollar bill into Tommy's hand, he beamed all over, as he held the money tightly in his hand, "Thanks mister! I hope you find her."

"Thanks to you Tommy, I will!"

Drew, went home and placed the groceries on the kitchen table, then grabbed a beer out of the refrigerator. As the drank his beer, he thought, 'God, she wouldn't go back to the island…..would she? Maybe she headed for Maine or

Vermont.' I'll go down to the dock and see Bill, first thing tomorrow.

While he laid in bed, he remembered how Gail, would snuggle into his arms and kiss his chest, while her hand gently stroked him. An involuntary groan escaped his lips, as he felt himself hardening, he spoke out load into the darkened room, "Wait for me baby, I'll find you soon!! He rolled over with a smile on his face and hope in his heart, for the first time in almost a month. With her name on his lips, he fell into a sound peaceful sleep.

During the last month, Gail had gained weight and she was tanned like a native. She, was happy and content, and had slept better in the last two weeks, this she credited to hauling wood and digging for clams and guaghogs which she loved and taking long exhausting walks.

She still couldn't think of Drew, without crying, for it still hurt to much to picture him with another woman She, could picture a woman clinging onto his arm, for he would be a great catch for any woman now.

"God!" she cried, out in her agony, "Why can't I be that woman?......I love him so." When this would happen, she would run along the beach until she was so exhausted that nothing else mattered.

Gail, had given Bill a letter to mail for her, to her sister, the last time he had dropped off wood and groceries to her, telling her not to worry, that she was well and happy. She received a letter back from Paul, telling her that Drew had been to the house looking for her. He also wrote, Drew really loves you Gail, don't throw a life time of happiness away. If he finds you, it's because he's done it on his own. We'll keep our promise to you, even if it kills us! She reread the letter, over and over again, when ever the going got rough.

Later that night, as Gail sat curled up in front of the fireplace, she could hear the wind howling outside, and the waves crashing angerily against the rocks........'God', She thought, 'I hope it doesn't storm before morning.'

Gail,sipped her drink and pulled the blanket up over her as she sat staring into the fire, that blew little puffs of smoke into the room everytime the wind blew a certain way. Gail thought of Drew going to her sister's house, and a warm feeling swept over her.

"Find me please......find me if you really love me!" she whistered, into the night, for this was her prayer for tonight. Curling up, even closer to the couch, she drew the blanket up under her chin, as the wind and the rain continued to howl outside.

When Drew, pulled up at the dock, he could see Bill, tying the boat up securely against the warf.

"Hi Bill!" he called out to him, above the wind.

"Hey Drew! Where the hell have you been keeping yourself lately?"

As they shook hands and laughed, Bill asked him to help him secure the boat, then they could go below, where it was warm.

"Here," Bill said, as he handed Drew the steaming mug of coffee,

"Drink this, it will warm you up. A short of whiskey in the coffee will do it every time!" he laughed, as he lifted the mug to his lips.

"Thanks Bill, I came to ask you if you had seen Gail lately?"

Bill turned, and pretended to be looking for something on the shelf, as he answered, "No....Why?" "Gail, left the hospital because of something stupid I did. I have to find her. I have to tell her that I'm sorry that I hurt her. I love her damn it!" Suddenly, his voice was almost to full of emotion to speak, as he turned and looked out the port hole saying, "God!......I miss her."

"I'm sorry to hear that Drew,...but I havn't seen her." He hated to lie to his friend like this, but it meant his job if he told anyone where Gail was.

Drew, knew his friend was lying, and he knew, he must hate doing it. That was alright, because he was even more determined now, that he was on the right track. As the two men put their empty mugs down, Drew smiled at his friend saying, "Thanks for the coffee Bill, I hate to leave but the wind is picking up and that means a storm is brewing. I want to get the helicopters into the hanger before it starts. Thanks again."

"So long Drew, I'm damn sorry I couldn't be more help to you." As Bill, watched Drew leave, he wanted to call him back and tell him that Gail was on the island,.............but he clamped his mouth shut, and kept silent. Then a curse broke from his mouth, "Damn it!....I hate this shit!"

When Drew started to get into his truck, the wind blew and out of the corner of his eye, over near the building, a tarp was flapping with the wind over something. "Damn," he said, to himself aloud, "Some poor sucker will have something ruined if that tarp blows off." As he ran to where it was his heart did a flip, then it began to beat faster and harder against his chest, as he recognized the red Camero, partly hidden beneath the tarp!

Just then, the rain started, and within minutes, it was coming down in torrents. By the time Drew reached his truck, he was soaked to the skin. He sat behind the wheel, wiping his face, not knowing if it was all rain, or a mixture of happy tears as well. "! knew I would find you sweetheart!" he cried out in relief, "please be there, don't leave!......I'm coming for you Darling....just as soon as I can get into the air!"

Sensing a bad storm was brewing, Drew headed for the air field, where Al, was already putting the chopper's in the hanger. As he pulled up beside the office, he jumped out of the truck and ran to where Al was trying to latch down a helicopter, that was under repair. This being done, they called it for the day, then headed for home, as the storm moved in with fury!

CHAPTER SIX

As the storm raged on into the night, Gail was suddenly awakened by a load clap of thunder, only to be followed by a crack of lightening, that lit up the sky, as well as her bedroom!

Gail sat up in bed, as her heart pounded faster and harder against her chest. Never, was she so frightened! She put her hands over her ears, and closed her eyes tightly, as she cried out into the night, "Please God, Make it stop!"

As the rain continued to crash against the window's, she dove under the covers, pulling the pillow and blankets up over her head, hoping they would block out the sound.

"Drew, where are you?....I need you soooooooo," She screamed, into the pillow, as she shook with fright. The loud claps of thunder drowned out her lonely cries into the night, as the storm showed no mercy for the frightened woman, as the storm raged on until dawn.

Many miles away, Drew woke to a clap of thunder that shook the house, shorting out the electricity, with the last bolt of lightening. Pulling on his shorts, and grabbing a flash light from the bed stand, he walked around the house to see if everything was all right.

He thought of Gail, knowing that she was on the island alone, and probably terrified, as this storm meant business! He prayed, that she was all right. He wanted desperately to be with her, just to hold her in his arms, until the storm passed. God......how he ached to hold her close to his heart, never had he felt this way about any other woman. Lighting up a cigarette and taking a long drag on it, he settled down in a chair facing the window, and waited for dawn to appear.

By morning, the electricity was back on, and while Drew was packing, he heard the radio announcer say, how it was one of the worst storms in years, and that the beaches were hit the hardest. Hearing this, only made him pack faster! He remembered, someone mentioning, 'winter clothes so, he packed his parker, his boots and gloves and anything else te would need. For if Gail was planning to be there for awhile......then so was he! For nothing she could possibly say or do would ever make him leave her........ever again!

Drew, went into the kitchen, and started putting food into a box, then he grabbed a case of beer from the back hall, and his last carton of cigerette's of the shelf, as he reached for the phone. He called Al, and told him of his plans to be away for a while, and that he would be in charge, until he returned, He also told Al, to meet him at the hanger, that he was to fly him to his destination, as he didn't want to leave the chopper on the beach. This way, if Gail told him to leave,....he couldn't! Drew smiled, as he grabbed the last of his personal items that he would need. As he closed the last bag he hoped he hadn't forgotten anything,...........for all he really needed was Gail.

When Drew arrived at the hanger, he met Al and told him of his plans. Then he went into the office to speak to Nancy, while Al started up the chopper. After telling Nancy, that he would see her, in what he guessed would be a couple of weeks or more, he handed her his house key, incase of an emergency, then he quickly kissed her cheek, as he turned to leave.

"Take care of yourself, and good luck!" Nancy called after him, as he ran toward the waiting helicopter.

As the helicopter lefted of the ground, a new fear crept into Drew's heart. What if she really didn't want to see

131

him......and what if she told him to leave? All kinds of crazy thoughts went through his mind, leaving him doubtful, that she would still feel the same way about him. Drew, felt as if he was breaking up inside, as crazy thoughts rampaged threw his mind. He could feel the sweat trickling down his back, and he hoped that his feelings didn't show.

Drew was so quiet, that Al, knew that he was having second thoughts about his trip. As he looked at his buddy, the sheen on his face told him everything. Looking straight ahead, Al spoke up, "Drew, if you need me, which I hope to God you don't, get in touch with Bill, and I'll be right here,"

Al said seriously. Then he smiled, saying, "Don't worry Pappy, everything will be all right between you too. I just know it."

As the island came into view, they could see the waves battering the shore line. "God!...There must had been one hell of a storm here! Just look at the island!" Al jelled over the sound of the engine, with a touch of anxiety in his voice.

"I hope Gail'a all right,.....I don't see her!" Al could hear the panic in Drew'a voice, as he prepared to land the chopper. Once the chopper was set down, they could feel the wind, and the smell of rain was still thick in the air, also the smell of smoke!

"Do you smell that?" yelled Drew, who couldn't keep the excitement out of his voice. "That means she's here, and she's all right!" Drew broke out with a smile that made Al shake his head, saying," Hell.....I hope I never fall in love, if this is what it does to a guy!"

After Drew had taken out all of his bags, Al looked at him with a knowing smile, "Come on, I'll help you carry your things to the top of the bluff. After that your on your own." laughed Al, as he bent down to pick up the case of beer and Drew"s duffel bag.

Once everything was piled all together, Al turned, and grabbed Drew by the shoulder's and hugged him for a quick minute, then he turned away quickly, saying," Best of luck Pappy, make her love you buddy!" Then he was gone.

Drew looked at the beach house, then picked up the box of food and headed for what he called home! The rest of his bags would be gotten later, for there was no one here to disturb them.

Drawing in his breath, he steeled himself against anything,Gail would say to him. Like it or not.......he was here to stay.......for he was determined to win back her love and respect.....even if it killed him.

When Gail awakened, the rain had stopped. She, quickly put on warn clothes, as she wanted to take a look around outside after breakfast, to survey any damage.

After eating, she went outside, taking the broom with her, as she wind had blown sand and debris all over the porch steps. After sweeping them off, she leaned the broom against the house, and headed for the beach.

"OHhhh NO!" she screamed, as she noticed the wharf was half torn away from the landing. Going nearer, she knew, she would have to repair it before Bill came back in January. But how?? Bill had made his last trip just two day's before. 'Thank God for that,' she thought, as she pushed her hair away from her face.

It was cold, and the wind bit through her jacket, as she walked with her head down against the wind. If she had only lifted her head, she would have seen Drew, as he entered the house.

Drew knocked, but receiving no answer, he opened the door and went into the kitchen, where he put the box of groceries down on the counter. Then, he went through the house calling, "Gail, where are you?" but to no avail. Knowing, that she must be on the beach, he headed for the door. Just as he reached for the door knob, he was greeted by Gail, who was about to open the door from the outside.

Gail let out a scream and turned to run, then she realized that the man in her kitchen was Drew! Stopping in her track, she turned, and he could see her breast's heaving with every breath she took. He had frightened her again, but God!....How beautiful she looked to him at this moment, with her hair flying wild, and her golden tanned face huddled inside of her collar of her jacket. At that moment, he wanted to gather her into his arms and never let her go. Instead, he opened the door and drew her inside.

"Drew! What are you doing here? she demanded,as she felt her throat tightening up.

"Gail, I had to see you,.....to talk to you." There's nothing to talk about, you said it all before!" She screamed at him, as she took a step backwards.

"Please Darling, let me explain. I was a damn fool! I love you Gail!" he pleaded once again.

"Why should I let you explain? You wouldn't let me explain things before! There was anger in her voice, and a hint of tears coming to her eyes, "how can you stand there and say, you love me, when you said you never wanted to see me again? She was crying now, and as he reached out to take her in his arms, she sobbed, "No! Don't touch me, just get in your helicopter and leave!" "I can't......Al, dropped me off, and I'm not leaving until you come with me!" "Well, you can't stay here!" she yelled, as she stomped past him into the living room. "Please Gail," he pleaded, as he followed her, "I'll stay out of your way if that's what you really want, but damn it!....We have to talk!"

As he followed her back into the kitchen, she turned, and looked at him for a moment, then spoke up in a sarcastic voice, "There won't be enough food for the two of us." She was grabbing at straws, and he knew it.

"I brought a few groceries from home. Don't worry, we'll manage, even if we have to fish for dinner." He argued back, as he jammed his fists into his pocket's.

Gail wanted to smile, as she had been doing that very thing right along, to be sure the meat would last. As she poured two mugs of coffee, she looked up at Drew,......" All right, you can stay, but don't try any funny business......understand?" She waited for an answer, as she held her ground.

God, but she was beautiful when she was mad. "O.k....you're the boss," he replied, as he reached for the mug of coffee. Well,.....At least he was inside the house, and that was step number one.

While Drew drank his coffee, he realized just how much he had hurt her, and he could tell she wasn't about to welcome him with open arms. He would just have to court her until she wanted and needed him just as much, as he needed her in his life.

While Drew was getting his duffel bag's, Gail,knew she had been hard on him, but.....she wanted him to feel what it was like to be hurt, and rejected, by the one you loved. What she really wanted to do, was to through her arms around him and never let him go, but her pride stood in her way. She, must be kidding herself, thinking she could ever let over him.....why....just looking at him made her weak all over, and she knew that she would always want and love him until the day she died.

While Drew helped her put away the groceries, they talked of the storm they had, the night before. "Storm!! You don't know what it's like unless you're here when it hits! I thought the house was going to blow away! The ocean was so wild it frightened me to death, just to hear the waves crashing on the beach. Never mind.....the thunder and the lightening!"

By the tone of her voice, Drew realized how frightened she had been, and for this, he cursed himself even more. "I only wish I could have been there with you."

"Me Too!" slipped out of her mouth, before she realized what she had said. Drew felt his heart pounding, at her two little words, he stood there smiling at her, until she left the room.

Later, that afternoon, Gail stood looking out the window, watching Drew, as he carried in an arm load of wood, toward the house. When he approached the back door, she ran to open it for him. As he stepped inside, his arm brushed against her breast, sending a shock through her, while the sent of cologne, sent her into a spin........ 'be still my heart', she said to herself, as she closed the door behind him.

"Boy, it's cold out there!" Drew exclaimed, as he rubbed his hands together, then put a few more logs on the fire. "I guess I had better make a fire in the back bedroom's" As he started to leave, Gail called out to him... "Hell....I may as well come with you and put clean sheets on your bed."

"Great, while your doing that, I'll start the fireplace in your room."

While Gail smoothed the sheets on his bed, she couldn't help remembering the last time they had shared this very bed with Drew. She began to get funny feeling in the pit of her stomach, as she remembered their making love. She could still picture him lying there, naked in all his splendor, and the look that he had given her made her heart race even now......just thinking about it! Suddenly, she realized that she was holding her breath, and that her hand had gone to her stomach, as if to stop the empty feeling.

With an ache in her heart, she hurried from the room, only to see Drew, still kneeling in front of the fireplace in her room, staring into the flames, as one who is in a trance. She wondered if he was remembering the good time too?

Not being able to stand there and watch him any longer, without throwing herself into his arms, she quickly turned and almost ran down the hall. Inside the kitchen, she leaned against the sink and held on, as she held her breath and closed her eyes tightly, as if to hold back any tears that threatened to fall. Why.....Oooooo...why....did she have to love him so much!

After Drew lit the fire in Gail's room, he glanced up and looked over at her bed. The covers were still all strewed all over the bed and on the floor. Proof that she had a terrible night. God....how he wished he had been with her. All he could remember, was how she had opened her arms to him, and welcoming him into her body, even when he was so badly disfigured.

Just, the thought of her knowing all along who he was and how he had looked, made him break out in a cold sweat, causing his heart to beat faster. He had a sudden urge to turn and run, before he hurt her again,.....but he loved her, and if this was to be his penance....then..so be it! He loved her, and he wasn't leaving until she knew it, and believed it.

God, how he needed to hold her ....to feel her in his arms......to chase all her fears and doubts away.......Drew took one more look toward the bed, then as he drew in a deep breath, while passing his hand over his face, to block out all visions of Gail in his arms and in his bed! Slowly he yurned, and headed for the kitchen, not knowing what was going to happen next, but full of hope.

Later that night, as he sat opposite Gail on the far side of the living room, he watched as she sat there calmly reading her book. She looked so small curled up in the chair, with her legs tucked up under her, while playing with a strand of hair, twisting and curling it, until he couldn't stand the silence between them any longer!

Drew, leaned forward in his chair and asked, with a heart felt sigh,

"Please Gail, can we talk?"

"Drew, please.....not now," she answered as she looked up at him over the rim of her book, "maybe some day soon, but please......don't say anything just now." Seeing that she was serious, he granted her wishes, and raiser both of his hands palms up, as he leaned back in his chair, "All right, anything you say."

It was early when Gail put her book aside, then stood saying," Good night Drew. It's been a long day and I didn't sleep very well last night."

"Sleep well", he answered, but before he had a chance to say Darlin, she had left the room. It was all he could do not to get up and fallow her and make her listen to him. Instead, he leaned back in the chair and tried to relax. After all....he was here, where he wanted to be, he could see her and feel her presence, and that was enough for now. He knew there was no hurry....for neither of them were going anywhere for awhile.

When Gail pulled the covers up under her chin, she was glad that Drew was here, and just a few feet away. She also knew that she would get a good nights sleep, knowing that he was in the house. So why, two hours later, was she still awake?.....Was it because he's in the house, or.....because he's just a few feet away????

Drew, woke the next morning to the sound of the shower running, he laid back in bed and waited to hear Gail leave the bathroom. When he heard her walking down the hall, he got out of bed and grabbed some clean clothes. The moment he stepped into the bathroom, all he could smell was her powder, that always aroused him. Even now...as he stood there taking in the sent of her, and thinking, "God, how much more of this can I take?" Gritting his teeth, he stepped into a cold shower to start his day.

"Good morning!" Drew called out, cheerfully, as he entered the kitchen. "Morning Drew, did you sleep well?" she asked as she poured the coffee, as if nothing was the matter. "Ya, how about you? I thought I heard you tossing around half the night." "Who me!.....Never! I slept like a baby."

Drew smiled, as he knew she was lying. "Well ......tell me what to do first, you must have a routine all figured out be now?" he asked, as he pushed his empty plate aside. "I have to earn my room and board. So......what will it be?"

"Well, first of all, you can look for any dead logs and chop them up for fire wood. There's a lot around the island, but they were to heavy for me to lift. They would burn much longer that the wood I've collected."

"What about the wood near the shed?" he had noticed it from the window, all neatly stacked, as he had put his empty mug in the sink.

"Oh, I'm holding that for the last thing to burn. Bill, brought a little wood over every trip he made. We'll need that when the snow comes.

Drew, pushed back his chair, and grabbed his jacket off the back of it, in one swift motion, then turned to leave.

"See you later beautiful!" was all she heard, as the door closed behind him.

Gail watched Drew disappear over the dunes, as she started doing the dishes. She kept remembering how he had looked at her during breakfast His eyes seemed to burn right through her, and she wondered, just how long she could keep him at bay.

After the dishes were done and the beds were made, she decided to go out and find Drew. She grabbed her jacket and put her hood up, and remembered to take her gloves, for the last time she was outside for any length of time, her hands froze. Remembering seeing Drew leave without his, she decided to look through his things for a paid. He was going to need them, this she knew for sure. They were easy to find, and she was on her way, with a small hatchet in her hand.

Gail could hear the sound of the ax, then she spotted Drew, cutting down a dead tree. She stood and watched as he swung the ax. He had such powerful shoulders and arms, that she was hipnotized by him. All she could see at that moment, was her in his arms,and how she loved the feel of them,when he would gather her close to him, just before he'de lower his head to kiss her. She could almost smell the scent of him, and the feel of his lips on her's. She, slowly closed her eyes, saying to herself, 'I've got to stop this right now'.

Suddenly, Drew sensed that he was being watched and as he turned, he saw Gail coming toward him with a smile on her face. "Did you come to help me?" he asked with a smile on his face, that melted and ice that was left around her heart.

"Yes, I came to help you pick up the small stuff," then as she stepped closer, she held out her hand to him," here are your gloves, I knew you'd need them. It get's damn cold out here after awhile."

"Thanks Gail," he replied, as he pulled the gloves on over his red numb fingers. Then his eyes traveled over her, he could see the changes that had taken place, she was in control of her life, and she loved the island, and all the work that went with it. Before him stood a happy, content woman, except when he looked deep into her sad eyes, which she kept turned away from his searching gaze.

They had worked silently side by side all morning, when Drew looked over at her, "Let's take a brake, I'm starved! How about you?" He was hot and sweaty, and as the sweat trickled down his face, it burned like hell,.......but he never said a word to Gail, as he didn't want her fussing over him,......for if she as much as laid a hand on him now, he wouldn't be able to keep his distance.

"All right. Let's carry some of the wood back with us, then I'll make lunch." Gail, turned and held out her arms for him to fill. With each piece of wood he stacked on her arms, he would stare into her eyes, as he fought the urge to grab her arms and kiss her until he had his fill! He, could feel the tension between them, and his heart felt as if it was slammed into his throat, as a soft moan escaped from his lips. Sensing what was happening between them, Gail blushed, as she lowered her eyes and turned away, as if she had read his thoughts.

Later, as they sat eating soup and sandwiches for lunch, Gail noticed how red Drew's face had gotten from the wind, and she knew that he must be in agony, but every time she lifted her eyes up from her dish, he deliberatly turned his away, so she couldn't tell what he was feeling. Damn,....she hated that look.....it was the same one she had seen more than once at the hospital! Only then, as a nurse she could tell him what to do!

After lunch, Gail asked if he would like clams for supper. Smiling at her, he agreed, for they were one of his favotite foods. As Gail watched Drew disappear from sight, through the kitchen window, she covered her face with her hands and moaned, as she didn't know how much longer she could go on like this......for she wanted and needed him ......now...as never before!

When drew made the last trip for the day, he was tired and dirty, and all he wanted was a cold beer and a hot shower, in that order. As he walked along the edge of the bluff, he looked down at the beach below, where he spotted Gail, on her knees, digging clams. At that moment she looked like a little girl to him, yet,.....he couldn't help but think, what a great wife she would make. She wasn't afraid to do any task, no matter how strenuous it would be. He knew she would always work beside her man, no matter what. He admired her for this, and wished he could tell her so.....but now was not the time or the place.

Drew had just finished washing up at the kitchen sink, when Gail came in bring a cold breeze with her. He took one look at her and started to laugh!

"Don't you dare laugh at me, Pappy!" She had used his nick name without thinking......and she felt the heat rushing to her cheeks and realized that she was blushing like a school girl.........Damn it! Why was she loosing herself control?

There she stood, wet and muddy past her knees, from kneeling on the wet sand, and her hair, wet and straggly from the salt air, and her nose was beet red from the cold wind. She looked a wreck, but to Drew, she was beautiful......so beautiful that she took his breath away! Holding the towel between his hands, he looked out the window, then turned with a smile, "I'm sorry Gail,.....but I can't help laughing.....you look so darn cute!"

"Cute!.......I'm half frozen to death, you idiot!"

Still laughing, he reached for the bucket of clams she was still holding, "Here give me the clams, and go take a hot shower.....like a good little girl!"

With her hands still shaking, she stood her ground and stared at him with fire in her eyes! "Great idea! ....I dug them, now you can cook them. How about that?" she fumed, as she stood there shivering. Then she turned and walked calmly out of the kitchen.

A hot shower was just what she needed, she was still chilled to the bone,but she was determined not to let Drew know this. Instead of dressing up, she put on her flannel pajamas and a pink woolly robe, then slipped her feet into her warm slippers. She then toweled dried her hair, until it fell softly around her shoulders. Looking at herself in the mirror, she saw a healthy, tanned woman staring back at her. Her breasts were full and firm inside her robe, and the sash that she tied, just below them, showed off her figure perfectly.

Speaking into the mirror, as she smoothed her hands down over her hips, "Little Girl!!...Am I??....We'll just see about that Mr. Hatfield!"

Taking one last look in the mirror, she smiled, as she tightened the sash on her robe one more time, and headed for the kitchen.

When Gail entered the room, the smell of clams got to her and she spoke with delight, "Boy, does it smell good in here!"

"How about a cold beer with them?" asked Drew, as he passed his eyes over her, only to let them rest on her bust, then to marvel at her hair, that gave off a scent of strawberry shampoo. Stepping closer to her, he smiled as he sniffed at her shoulder and whispered into her hair, "you smell good! too!"

Gail's heart skipped a beat, as she felt his warm breath against her neck, as he held the chair for her to sit. Noticing that he had the table set, and everything was undercontrol, she asked, "So.....how was your first day here? Do you think you'll like being here for two months?" hoping, she had shaken him up a bit, she took a sip of beer, as she waited for his answer.

"I'm going to like it just fine, ".......if I don't break my back first, he thought to himself. He was already getting stiff,and his hands were begining to blister.......and this was only the first day!

They ate in silence for a few minutes, as the clams were fresh and tasty. Gail could feel Drew's eyes on her every time she put a nother clam in her mouth. She looked up at him and his eye's were smiling back at her, He had the begining of a smile coming to the corners of his mouth, as he thought,...God! Hurry and eat thoes clams before I explode! He didn't know how much longer he could keep up this pretense,....he knew she had to be the first one to make the first advance....so ....what the hell was keeping her from it!?

As Gail watched Drew, she could see his mood change and she wanted to scream at him that he had hurt her, and not to do it again! But ...once again, her pride stood in her way.

While they finished eating they talked about what had to be done on the dock. They decided that they would hall

144

wood in the mornings, and work on the dock in the afternoon's, as it would be warmer then. They agreed on just
about every thing, and this led Drew to think that he was
beginning to make a little headway with Gail.

Gail, pushed back her chair and began to gather up the
dishes, saying "I'll do up these dishes while you fix the
fireplaces in the bedrooms, then we'll have a drink and
relax....if that's all right with you?"

"Sounds fine with me." When Drew got up from the
chair, she could see that he was beginning to get stiff. She
knew he hadn't done any out door work like this for some
time, and she remembered how she had felt the first week
that she was here. She had ached all over, but the blisters on
her hands had been the worst. She knew he was hurting, and
that he had to much pride to ask for help.

When Drew, placed the last log on the fire, he turned to
see Gail coming towards him with a tube of salve and some
bandages. He dropped down into the easy chair with a
groan, as she knelt down in front of him, and asked to see
his hands.

"Look Gail, you don't have to do this." "I know I don't,
"she whispered, as she took his out stretched hands in her's,
turning them palms up. She pulled in her breath, when she
saw the angry blisters, while she opened the tube of salve,
which she gently smoothed over his palms and fingers. He
flinched, once or twice, and she could feel the heat of his
hands through the salve. "There, maybe they'll feel better
now," she said, as she wrapped them in gauze. As she
started to rise, Drew took hold of her arm and looked up at
her through loving eyes, "Thanks Darlin, they feel better
already."

Sitting back, Drew watched as Gail busied herself
making them a drink, and putting a tape on. All, he could

145

think of was Gail, how her back and hands must have hurt,.........and how she had no one to care for her, as she had just done for him. How, she had never once mentioned how hard it must have been for her to do a man's work. He, suddenly realized, that there was a lot about this woman, that he was just finding out. Knowing this, only made him love and respect her, even more......

Gail, watched Drew fall asleep in the chair, as she slowly sipped her drink. Suddenly, she wanted to go to him and kiss his pain away. She loved him so much, that just seeing his muscles move under his thin sweater, turned her on emotionally. She desired this man so much, that she knew, she would have to be careful, or she would say to hell with revenge and throw herself at him. Never.....had she wanted a man so completely as she wanted Drew. Snuggling down in her chair, she was content, just to watch him sleep.

It was ten- thirty, when Gail nudged Drew, "Drew, wake up and go to bed. It's late." As he pushed himself slowly out of the chair, he grabbed his back with a moan, and walked stiffly from the room.

Later, as Gail went around shutting off lights, she thought of Drew, and as she went by his bedroom, she stopped and listened, then as she was about to leave, she heard him moan softly then the bed creaked, as he must have turned over. Gail headed for the bathroom and the medicine cabinet, where she took a tube of Ben-gay and headed back to Drew's room. When she knocked on his door, a muffled voice answered, "Come in." As she slipped into his room, she could see his outline on the bed, from the moonlight that filtered in through the window. Drew, rolled over and tried to sit up, asking," Gail, what's the matter?"

"Nothing Drew, I know your back is hurting,..... so if you let me rub this salve in your back, you'll feel much better in the morning." While she talked, she had moved closer to his bed. Drew hurt to much to argue with her, and he knew all to well, that a nurse always wins! Without thinking he replied, "Sure High- pockets, do your thing," as he rolled over on to his stomach.

Gail turned on the light, as she sat down on the edge of the bed beside Drew, and pulled the covers back. Then she squeezed out a generous amount of Ben-gay and began to rub it in. As she gently began to massage his back, he made noises that made her smile in spite of herself. It felt good to feel his smooth skin under her finger tips, and she lingered as long as she dared.

"OH, don't stop, that feels sooooo.....good," he sighed, as the touch of her hands had begun to turn him on. He felt himself hardening, as he tried to gain control of his feelings. As he slowly rolled over, he brought up one knee, so she wouldn't see how much she had effected him.

"Do you have a tee-shirt handy?" she asked, as she turned away.

"Ya, in the top drawer." He watched, as she walked across the room, and the swaying of her lovely bottom under her robe, only made his temperature rise, as he adjusted the sheet once more!

Gail helped him into his tee-shirt, and as she pulled it down over his back, his arms automatically went around her. For a moment, neither of them spoke, as there eyes locked. Gail swallowed, then licked her lips, as she held her breath.....hoping that he would kiss her. Drew, had the desire to pull her close and kiss those beautiful lips, that looked moist and inviting,.....God,....but she felt good to him! Gail, pushed herself away from him and stood up, putting the light out at the same time.

"Good night Pappy,....try to sleep"

"Night, High- Pockets, I'm sure I won't after this!"

Back in her own room, Gail sank into bed, with a little moan of regret. She wanted him, and she knew he was feeling the same desires as she, but......she couldn't give in to them..........Not yet! She only hoped that she would have the strength to hold out for a few more days.

"Oh God," she sighed," if he puts his arms around me again,......I'm lost! "Rolling over, she pulled the covers up, and with a smile on her lips for the first time, in a very long while, she fell asleep

Drew, had been on the island for over a week, and now the ax in his hand felt like a part of him. Even the back aches had disappeared, and he began to feel at peace with himself. He knew it was time to talk with Gail, but....he didn't know quite how to start. Things were going smoothly between them and he didn't want anything to change that.

All he wanted, was to be able to hold her in his arms once in a while, without her pulling away. He knew nature would take it's course, and she would have to be the one to make the first advance,.....but, damn it.....he didn't have to like it!! Something had to change, for it was getting harder and harder for him to keep his hands off her!

As he finished working on the wharf for the day, he wondered why Gail hadn't come down to watch him work, as she usually did in the afternoon. With this in mind, he gathered up his tools and headed back to the house.

When Drew entered the kitchen, the aroma of food cooking was wonderful. He peaked inside the oven where a roast was cooking, with brown potatoes and onions piled high around it. Then lifting the lids of the sauce pans he saw butter nut squash and green beans. He also noticed that the table was set with candles and wine glasses, and it looked like he was in for a treat. He smiled, and hoped that he would be a part of the dessert ………much later!

He whistled, as he headed for the shower, then as he reached Gail's room, he hesitated, then knocked.

"Yes?"

"Gail, Am I supposed to dress for supper?" he asked, as he leaned against the wall, with a ray of hope in his heart, that maybe she had forgiven him…..

"Yes" came softly through the door.

"O.K babe, anything you say," he called back over his shoulder, as he hurried toward the bathroom. Once inside, he rested his head against the mirror, for there it was again, the smell of her powder! It was driving him mad! Her sent was every where, he could feel himself harden, as he stepped into the cold shower. Later with a towel draped around him, he hurriedly shaved, then walked across the hall to his room to dress.

A few minutes later, he was dressed in his one and only dress slacks and his best sweater. Looking down at his feet, he was glad that he had worn his dress shoes to the island.

While Gail listened to Drew showering, she hurriedly slipped into her green wool dress, that left nothing to the imagination. She put her hair up into a french twist, then put on her gold earrings, as she slipped into her brown loafers. Damn….she wished she had her high heels with her! Turning, she looked at her reflection in the mirror, and hoped that Drew, would like what he saw. After all…..hadn't she dressed just for him?!

When Drew entered the kitchen, Gail was putting wine on the table. She looked up, just as he was looking her over

149

from head to toe. "God Gail, your beautiful," he murmured, as he devoured her with his eyes. "You look terrific," he whispered into her hair, as he held her chair for her. once she was seated, he sat down, only to stare at her with love in his eyes.

"You look pretty spiffy yourself," she stated softly, as she watched his mouth break into a smile. OH....how she wanted to feel those lips on her's again!

While they ate, they decided that this was the best meal that they had eated since Drew's arrival. "I've been holding the roast for a special occasion, "she stated, as she started to blush.

His reart gave a leap, and he tried to keephis body under control, as he asked, "What occasion it that?"

"My birthday!......It's today!

"Your birthday......well, Happy Birthday."

Then she asked, with a smile, "When is your's?" "March twelfth, I'll be thirty-three," he answered, as he realized, that they never knew each others age, not that it mattered a hell of a lot. He'd love her no matter how young or old she was.

Getting up from the table, Gail said, "I've made a cake, but I didn't have any candles,.....so I used a match instead." When she placed the cake on the table, they both laughed, to see one lonely candle burning in the middle of it. Drew looked across the table at her saying, "Make a wish Honey, today is your day! "

Gail looked into his smiling eyes, that she loved so much, then puckered up...and blew out the match. Her wish was for him to make passionate love to her, here and now! Suddenly, she felt herself blushing at her thoughts, and she quickly lowered her eyes, but not before Drew spotted just a hint of the old flame that he loved so much. While pushing back his chair, he held out his arms, and asked her to dance.

Nodding yes, she went into his arms willingly. He drew her close to his chest, and laid his cheek against her hair, as he asked, just above a whisper, "May I kiss the birthday girl?"

The way she offered her lips to him, was all the answer he needed. As he lowered his lips to her's. he noticed that her's were slightly parted, as if waiting for him. He kissed her lovingly, until he felt her body pressed against the length of him. Feeling himself getting aroused, he ran his tongue over her lips, then deepened the kiss, as he reviled in the taste of her. With a little moan, he pulled away looking down at this precious woman in his arms. As her eyes slowly opened, there was a look of surrender. At that moment he wanted to make love to her, to kiss and taste every inch of her, to become one with her,.......but instead he continued dancing, while holding her captive in his arms.

Gail sensed that he was going to kiss her, and when he did, she wanted to hold on to him forever, for nothing that had happened in the past mattered now. Suddenly, she realized that he had stopped kissing her, and that they were still dancing. Sick at heart, she damned herself, take your medicine she said to herself, you made the conditions and now you know where you stand!........Damn him anyway!.....He's going to make me make the first move!

When the music ended, Drew stepped back, still holding her in his arms, and asked, "you're a great dancer, why didn't you ever do something with it, instead of becoming a nurse?"

Before answering him, she led him into the front room, and settled him down on the couch with a drink in his hand. Then she settled in on the other end of the couch with her feet up, and a large drink in her hand for moral support, before she started to talk.

"I don't know,.....I always loved to dance, but I felt I would be going no where with it. Then the war broke out. By then, I was in nurses training and decided to join up. I was twenty-one and I thought I was going to heal the world. It didn't take me long to see the real world, and all the pain and suffering that was in it." She took a large gulp of her drink, then cleared her throat, as she looked up at the ceiling before she could speak again. I was stationed on a hospital ship, when they flew in a hole platoon of men that had been burnt,.....by what I called a blow torch!" Her eyes suddenly filled with tears, and Drew wanted to reach out and comfort her, but he didn't make a move, as this was the first time she had opened up to him. "When my tour was over, I came home to stay with my sister and her husband."

There was compassion in her voice, as she continued talking. "Paul and I would talk for hours about burn patients, and the latest methods that were in use. One day I went to visit the hospital with Paul, and when I saw the children,......as well as a number of veterans that needed me, I knew right away, this was my destiny. So,....I started working that very next week."

While Drew listened, he could feel the love and compassion she had for others, and he couldn't help but ask, "God Gail, how can you stand to see so much pain and suffering al the time, day after day?"

"It wasn't easy. there were times. that I had to leave the ward for a while. Sometimes, ...crying helped.....but.... what really bothered me the most......was seeing the children suffer."

Drew, could tell that it was difficult for Gail to be telling him all of this, but the words were just rolling out of her, and he knew she needed to talk. As she talked, hereached over the back of the couch and took hold of her hand in his, while gently tracing little circles on the back oh her hand with his thumb.

"Some of the children never made it, while others are so badly scared and disfigured, that they will probably spend most of their lives in and out of hospitals. These children were never ugly to me......to me, they were frightened, helpless children, that were far away from home, and needed a lot of love, and someone to chase their fears away. This, I tried to do.....God! What courage they have.....There was a little boy that I got attached to," a little sob broke from her lips, as she tried to keep control of her feelings, "and when he died, ...I just fell apart........That's when Paul, and Philip, sent me to this island. They told me, no one would be here, but me! So ....I came, and you know the rest." She closed her eyes, as she had let him see into her most inner feelings for a short while. She brushed a lonely tear that ran down her face, as she raised her eyes to look at him.

"Ya," He answered softly, "I came and accused you of imposing on my privacy. My face was such a mess, that I didn't want anyone to see it. I came here to prepare myself for more surgery, and I found you! I fell for you the minute I saw you,.....but you were out of my reach....and I knew it! I never meant to make love to you, and then leave,.... but...I loved and needed you so much, that I couldn't help myself."

As Drew continued talking, Gail sat up, putting her legs down off the couch, enabling him to move closer to her, as he talked. Drew spent the evening telling her how he had been injured while in the service. He left out the terrible ordeal he had gone through when his helicopter crashed in Vietnam, of how he had screamed in agony, as his uniform was set ablaze by the explosion that followed the crash, or the pain and suffering he had endured over the last few years, as his body tried to heal itself with the doctor's help.

Gail, listened quietly and let him talk, as she knew, what he must have gone through, as she had taken care of so many service men that had been badly burnt. She knew, how hard it was for him to open up to her, she also knew, that he had to get it off his chest,.... and the best way for that, was for him to talk about how he felt.

"Gail, when you came into my room that first night, I wanted to disappear from sight, but when you leaned down and kissed me,....well...damn it!! I needed you too." His voice had become husky, and at times it was hard for him to speak, "I'm only human,...no....It's more than that, I loved you and I wanted you as a man wants the woman he loves!" He held on to her hand, as he continued talking, "when I left you the first time, I never thought I'd ever see you again. You were so beautiful, and I was so ugly." Gail tried to say, "No you weren't!" but he stopped her with his finger on her lips. "I didn't want us to be known as the beauty and the beast......I had to let you go! Can you understand how I felt?"

"Yes Drew, I can. I never expected to see you again, and I couldn't tell you that I had seen your face. That it didn't matter to me. That I loved you just the same." Then smiling, she said," Did you know that I thought you were a gangster of so kind on the run!?"

"No! Really!?"

"Yes! Until I found out why you were always hiding from me, I thought you were afraid that I'd recognize you, for a crime of some sort!" Then he laughed, as she had never heard him laugh before.

Moving closer, so that their hips were touching, he became serious once more, saying, "The doctor's told me about the nick names, and how you really didn't know it was me at first. I guess, I was mad, because I loved you so much. Then when High -Pockets came along, I trusted her with my life. What pain I had, I didn't want you to ever see.....but High-Pockets, was my nurse....and she could handle it. then when High- Pockets, stopped coming around, I got mad as hell!!.........Because we had become such good friends. That friendship, I didn't want to lose! That's why, when I saw that you were one in the same person,....I blew my mind!.....I felt betrayed!"

As she leaned a little closer to him, she softly said, "I know Darling, and I'm so sorry for deceiving you. All I wanted was for you to get back to normal, and to start living again. I knew, after that day, that it was all over between us. I also knew, that some girl would come along and grab a great catch like you right away.......I was so happy for you, but miserable thinking of another girl ever being in your arms." Her mouth began to quiver,and he took her in his arms and kissed her before the first tear could fall.

"Please Darling, Don't cry," he whispered against her lips, "I had a terrible time trying to find you, and all I know now is, that I never want to leave you again." With that he pulled her against him and kissed her with all the pent up emotion, that couldn't be held back.

Gail, suddenly became alive in his arms. Answering each kiss with her own longing. As he deepened the kiss, she opened up for him,as he slipped his tongue into her mouth to mate, and tease with her own. Her breathing changed and she answered him stroke for stroke, searching and tasting, until she felt his hand traveling up and down her back, while his other hand caressed her breast, through her dress. She let out a little moan, as he slid his lips down the side of her neck, and on to the hollow of her throat.

Oh God! she thought, how I've longed for this!

As she relaxed on the couch, in a lying down position, she pulled him down to her, until her breast's were molded against his chest, as a groan escaped his lips, he swung his leg's up so they would be lying side by side. As he pulled her in closer, he could feel the heat of her body, all soft and warm and inviting. The way she snuggled in closer to his hips, he knew she could feel what she was doing to him, with her lips and now her hands. First they had been in his hair, and now she was trailing them down his chest and beyond, to the bulge behind his zipper. Her breathing became difficult, as she felt her desire rising to match his.

"Oh Gail," he murmured, into her shoulder, "I love you and want you.........but, not like this. Not just because we're feeling sorry for one another, or that it's great sex every time we're together. I want you to want me the same way that I want you! I want you to marry me." He,was holding her and talking in a husky voice, as he found it difficult to speak. "I want to spend the rest of my life with you. I want to raise a family like other people, and have all the good things in life. Most of all.....I want to make love to you for the rest of my life! I'm sorry,.....but I can't play this cat and mouse game any longer. When you feel the same way.....come to me, and I'll never let you go."

Gail, felt him, release her and start to get up........she was so stunned, that she just looked up at him, through blurred eyes with her mouth open, as if to say something, but no words would come. Her lips trembled, and she felt as if her heart had been ripped out of her chest. What had she done?....Didn't he know that she loved him above everything else in this whole cockeyed world!?

By the time she could speak, he had gotten up and was now putting logs onto the fire, that would last until morning. Then, as she watched, he turned his back to her and walked from the room........leaving her alone once again. Gail, put the lights off and walked as if in a daze to her room. There puzzled and bewildered, she crept into a cold lonely bed....only to toss and turn, as she cried deep into the night.

It had been a terrible week for both of them, as the tension between them was becoming unbearable. Gail wished that she could turn back the clocks, and do things differently, and Drew, wishing that he had kept his mouth shut, as he loved her and wanted her on any terms! They both realized that one of them would have to do something soon, as they could feel a wall building between them. But ....witch one would it be?

During the night, the first snow storm hit, and now they had to stay inside. The wind was picking up speed, and the waves were pounding the surf, sending up a spray that was fascinating to watch.

The two lovers sat playing cards, both acutely aware of each other, as the sound of the storm cut through the silent room. They had been plating cards most of the day when Drew looked up, with a sheepish grin on his face, hoping to break the ice by saying, "Hay....sweetheart," in a sexy drawl, "how about a little strip polka!?" "Are you crazy!" she fired back at him.

"O.k....if you don't want to….. but it was a good idea!" He could picture her taking off her clothe, one piece at a time. He could picture her body all tanned, except for the white of her breasts He wanted her so badly, that just the thought of her standing nude before him, made him suddenly hard with desire. All of a sudden he was brought back to reality by Gail saying." Drew, stop daydreaming like that! I can read your mind!" Just seeing him smile again made her feel warm all over. For each time she looked at him, she could feel herself blush, and she would lower her eyes, for she read him like a book. She was happy, thinking that everything was going to be all right, then suddenly, out of the blue, Drew declared, in a sarcastic tone of voice," I didn't realize that I was being that obvious. I'll try not to smile, the next time I'm thinking of you. "Suddenly.....the invisible wall was between them once more.

During the night, five inches if snow had fallen, and the temperature had dropped drastically It was as if someone had spread a blanket of white over the island. They had taken a couple of chairs and now sat looking out the window and listening to the storm. The sound of the raging sea, and the pounding of the surf, as it crashed onto the shore held them spellbound for hours. Knowing it was getting late, Gail, turned to Drew and asked, "Would you prefer a hamburger or chops for supper?" "I don't care, either will do. I'm not hungry anyway."

Gail, noticed that Drew had become moody, and she wanted to cheer him up.....but she kept saying the wrong things. then, a terrible thought past her nind.....mabe he was having second thoughts about them, for he hadn't tried to kiss or touch her since the night of her birthday. Was she loosing him now....after all they had been through together? No!....She wouldn't let this happen. He meant the world to her and she would find away to tell him just that! Just the thought of loosing him made her stomach tighten and she felt sick at heart. For never to feel his arms around her filled her with remorse and fear. She couldn't let this happen! Not now....when she needed him and wanted him so desperately!

That evening, as Drew sat by the fire reading a book, Gail, couldn't stand the silence any longer. He had to speak to her or she would scream! Going to where he sat, she knelt down in front of him, and gently took the book away from him. Looking up, he asked, "What are you doing now?"

Looking into his eyes, that looked so full of pain and doubt, she had to swallow her pride, as she placed her hands on his knee's. and hoped he'd understand what she was about to say. "Drew......why haven't you talked,or fooled, with me these last few days? I thought we had something pretty special going between us."

"I did too, but it can't be all one sided,....I make a pass at you and you turn away. I can't take any more of this! He leaned forward, to look into her eyes, with a sadness that he could not hide. "I love you Gail, but you have to want me and love me too! Christ!....I'm only human. I can't be in the same house with you,....day after day and act like brother and sister. I've tried to keep my hands off you, for your sake. I've waited for you to come to me....to make the first move,.....but you haven't."

"I know Drew, and I'm sorry. I don't want it to be thin way either. I love you Drew, I always have, so what's the matter?" As she spoke, fear crept into her heart, fear...that she was loosing him, fear that this was to be the end.

Drew, took both her hands in his, as he wrestled with his feelings, "Look.....since we've been together, I've learned a lot about you that I didn't know before. maybe I'm not the right man for you. Maybe it's pity you feel,.....I don't know any more! I've tried to please you, but you've drifted away from me. Maybe your afraid of being hurt again....I don't know....All I know is that I can't blame you for that."

Norma Marie

Gail, could feel the tears starting, and she had a lump in her throat, which made it almost impossible to speak. "Are you telling me.... that you don't feel the same any more?" Her heart was breaking, and she knew, she was going to cry if she stayed there a moment longer. She, quickly stood up and turned to go, then before he could answer, she stopped to say, "I hope you find the right girl someday." Then she turned and fled to her room, to close the door and cry., while part of her was dying.........What a fool she had been.....She wanted him, but on her own terms, ...and now it was all over. She cried so hard that she thought her heart would break. Sitting up, she knew that she had to get out of the house for a while,...snow or no snow!

Gail, waited until she heard Drew's bedroom door close, then she tip-toed past his door, to the kitchen. There she pulled on her boot's and put on her jacket, as she slipped out the back door.

The wind was cold and blustery, coming off the water, and it hit her, as she put up her hood and pulled on her gloves, but,....the cold bit right through them, leaving her chilled to the bone. With her head down, against the wind, she walked to the edge of the bluff, and stood looking out over the ocean and trying to figure out what she had done wrong,...when only a few days ago he had wanted to make love to her. As the wet snow whipped at her face, she remembered back to her birthday, and Drew saying, "I want you to marry me, and when you feel the same way too....come to me, and I'll never let you go!"

Then it hit her......that was it!!...He had been waiting for her to come to him all along! He wanted to marry her!! "Oh Drew Darling," she shouted, into the wind, "I'm coming, I love you!"

In her haste, as she turned, she slipped and lost her footing and tumbled over the edge. Gail screamed, as she felt herself falling, only to land with a thud, and to roll and tumble down the slope to the rocks below.

The last thing she remembered, was screaming as she fell,....a sickening thud,...then nothing.....

Back at the house, Drew, lay there staring at the ceiling, unable to sleep. He didn't want to lose Gail, just because of stubborn pride. "Damn it!....I love her, and I'm sick of playing these silly games!" He muttered, out loud himself, as he got up and pulled his pants on. "I know she loves me.......It's that stubborn pride of her's that's keeping us apart!" He was still muttering to himself, as he headed for Gail's room.

He knocked softly, as he didn't want to frighten her. Then, when there was no answer, he turned the door knob and stepped inside. Once inside, he whispered, "Gail Darling, I'm sorry." All the while he moved closer to the bad. Getting no answer, he snapped on the lamp beside her bed. To his suprise, he saw that her bed was messed up, but, that it hadn't been slept in. He turned, and ran out of the bedroom, calling, "Gail where are you?" When he reached the kitchen, he noticed that her boot's and jacket were missing. Panic filled his heart, as he raced back to his room to dress. While putting on his sweater, he thought he heard a scream,......that made his hair stand on end. "Gail!.....Oh God!" he cried out, as he ran back to the kitchen, where he pulled on his boots and slipped into his parka. Then grabbing the flash light off the refrigerator, he raced out the back door. All he knew at that moment, was that he had to find her, and find her fast!!

As he stepped off the porch, and started to run, he slipped and fell into the cold wet snow. Getting up, he

161

swore at himself for falling. As he headed toward the bluff, he had to lean into the wind, as the wet snow stung his face,.....like a thousand razor blades. He tucked his head, into his arm, that he held up to protect himself, as he flashed the flashlight beam, onto the ground ahead of him.

"Gail, where are you!?" he called, over and over again, into the wind. He, was about to loose control, when suddenly........he, saw her foot print in the wet snow. "Thank God." he prayed, out loud. His heart stopped, beating for a moment, when he saw that her prints led to the edge of the bluff, where the snow had fallen away.

"Oh God .....No!.... Gail!" he shouted, over and over again, as he started down the side of the bluff, sliding on his bottom, as not to tumble down. Half way down, he spotted her yellow jacket. He, quickly flashed the light on her,......she looked so small lying there, sprawled out near the rocks below. "Gail!....Gail!! I'm coming!" he called, out to her, as he hurried down, to where she layed so still.

Kneeling down beside her, he called her name once again, then getting no answer, began to feel for any broken bones, He thanked God, that there were none. He, gathered her up in his arms and started to walk back up the beach, to where the path ran along the side of the bluff.

Drew's leg's felt like dead weight, as hiswet pants were begining to freeze. He knew, he had to hurry, as the wind was bitter cold, and they were both wet to the skin. His face and hands were already numb, but he held onto his precious cargo that he held so tightly in his arms. Suddenly, he tripped and fell, only to land in the wet snow, and slide back a few feet. As he picked Gail, up into his arms again, he knew he couldn't carry her this way. He stopped, and put her over his shoulder, in a fireman's hold, hoping that he would be able to see where he was stepping. When Drew reached the top, he fell to his knees from exaustion, never letting Gail out of his arms, that now ached, from the weight of her.

"Please God," he prayed, as he lifted her once more onto his shoulder, "let me make it to the house," Suddenly the house came into view and Drew tried to hurry, but his legs just wouldn't work" "Damn it!!.....don't quit on me now!....I know you're there, even if I can't feel you!!"

Once inside the house, Drew kicked the door closed behind him, then laid Gail down on the couch. He, quickly stocked up the fire, then returned to the unconscious girl. Seeing her lips blue, he hurriedly began to remove her boots and jacket. Seeing that she was wet through to the bone, he quickly removed all of her clothing, and wrapped her into the blanket, that was draped over the couch. Then he quickly kicked off his boots and dropped his jacket and pants where he stood, as they were frozen solid.

He, went back to Gail, who was now shivering, and started to rub her feet and hands, not caring that he was cold and half naked, or that his face was hurting like hell. He pleaded, frantically, for her to open her eyes, to talk to him. He knew, he had to get something hot into her, but how....and what?!

Then he had a flash back, of when he was a little boy, how his mother would take him to bed with her and hold him close, to warm him up. "Thanks Mom!" he said,aloud, as he scooped Gail, up in his arms, blanket and all. He bent and grabbed the bottle of brandy off the coffee toble, as he hurried to his room. once there, he removed the blanket from Gail and checked her for broked bones and cuts, that he might have missed earlier. The only thing visible was a lump on her forehead, that was already turning blue, where she must have hit her head,when she fell. There would be more bruses and sore muscles by tomorrow, this he knew.

Pulling back the covers, he lowered, Gail's, nude body into his bed, then he removed the rest of his clothing with one quick sweep. As he stood there shivering, he took a couple of good swigs of brandy out of the bottle, then climbed into bed and stretched out, drawing the blanket's up over the two of them. He, could feel the brandy warming his insides, as he reached out to draw Gail close to his side. Once he felt the coldness of her body against the length of his, he began to rub her back and arms, only to return to her icy bottom, then to her thighs. He even rubbed his feet against her's hoping to warm them.

After what seamed like hours, he felt the warmth coming back into her body, this alone gave him hope. "That's my girl," he whispered, as he kissed her cool lips until they were warm beneath his. Still,....her body did not respond to his. Suddenly, he was frightened, that something serious had happened to Gail. As an uncontrollable sob burst through his lips, he gathered her closer, pleading, close to her ear, "Darling, don't leave me! ....I can't live without you!"

Drew knew, that he was wetting her face with his tears, but he could no longer control his feelings. Panic had taken over, and he realized how close he had come to loosing her. His chest hurt, and he felt as if his heart was breaking, as he remembered all that he had said to Gail. He felt sick with remorse at what he had said, when all of a sudden, he felt a hand move over his heart then slowly up to his shoulder, then around his neck, only to hold his head closer to her's.

Realizing Gail had come to, he whispered into her hair, "It's all right Darling, I'm here, and I'm not going anywhere with out you." Drew, raised himself up on his elbow, so that he could look into her beautiful eyes, that were now full of tears. "Drew.....is it realy you?" she mumbled, as she muffeled a sob, "I thought I had lost you.....then I remembered what you had said to me......I wanted to run back and tell you that I loved you! ....That I wanted to marry youuuu too! "Drew, drew her close while running his hand over her hair, as he whispered, "Shhhhh.....It's all right...I understand."

Clinging to him, she sobbed into his shoulder, "I must have lost my footing when I turned around. Then, when I fell, I thought I'd never see your handsom face again," then she hugged him tightly against her, as she let the tears fall.

Drew, held her while he kissed her hair, her face, that tasted salty from her tears, then back to her lips that welcomed his. Drew knew, that he had to calm her down, that she needed rest now, more than ever. He, rolled over and got out of bed, not caring that he was stark naked, and went into the bathroom, where he found a glass, which he brought back to give Gail a sip of brandy. He, sat on the edge of the bed and gently helped Gail to sit up.

She made a terrible face, as she gulped down the brown liquid, then she layed back, as she felt the warmth of the liquor taking over.

Never had she looked so beautiful to him as she did sitting there with her hair mussed up and her lips still swollen from his kisses, and her bare breast's uncovered for his eyes only. God, how he wanted to take her into his arms and make wild passionate love to her. To kiss her from head to toe, but he knew he would have to wait until later.

Drew, checked her forehead once more, before he slipped into bed beside her. When he reached to put out the light, he noticed that it was almost daylight. Rolling over, he gathered Gail close to him, spoon fashion as he told her to go to sleep, for she would always be save in his arms. Soon, Gail fell asleep locked in his arms, exhausted, but happy and content.

Drew waited until he could hear her breathing softly, and knew that she was asleep, before he let himself relax. Under his hand that held her breast so gently, he could feel her heart beating strong and steady. He smiled, as he kissed her shoulder, then drew her a little closer, as he closed his eyes in slumber.

The next morning, when Drew awakened, he felt a warm soft body pressed against his. He didn't have to open his eyes to know that it was Gail…..and not a fragment of his imagination. He could feel the steady beat of her heart in his hand, that held her breast so tenderly. 'God,' he thought, how I love this woman! 'He, loved everything about her. Her sent, her softness, the way she sighs, and calls out his name as they make love, but most of all, he loves the way she makes him feel whole again, as well as loved and needed. For all these reasons and more, he would always love her. He, gently kissed her shoulder,….then slipped carefully out of bed, as not to awaken her.

The floor was cold under his feet as he knelt to start the fire in the fireplace. Soon the flames were coiling around the logs and he could feel the heat starting to flow into the room. He shivered, as he turned to take one last look at Gail sleeping before he hurried into the bathroom to take a hot shower

This alone warmed him up and he felt like a new man, as he stood there shaving with a towel wrapped around his waist. After combing his hair, he went back into the bedroom to dress.

As he sat on the side of the bed to pull his briefs on,,,,,,he felt a soft hand touch his shoulder, while at the same time, a pair of soft lips trailed kisses up his back to the base of his neck, where Gail, placed a kiss as she drew him back into her embrace Laying her head against his back, she whispered, in a sexy voice, "and where do you think your going my Darling? "...as her hand began to roam over his chest and lower to clasp his manhood. When her hand came in contact with him, a groan escaped his lips, as his desire for her became over powering. "God, Gail, what you do to me."...he gasped, as he felt himself hardening under her touch.

"Please Drew," she whispered, against his ear that she bit so gently, "make love to me...now...I need you so!" Turning, he clasped his arms around her, as his mouth clamed her's, in a kiss that left them both trembling. As he deepened his kiss, she parted her lips for his tongue to enter, to taste and tease her with the excitement of what was to come. "UMmmmmm," he sighed, as he slipped once again under the covers with the woman of his dreams.

Later, lying side be side, exausted but truly happy, Gail, whispered into his shoulder, "remember the day High-Pockets said, "if you wished real hard our dreams of love would come true?" "Ya Sweetheart, I remember," he answered, as he drew her closer while kissing her hair. "Well it has, I'll always love you Drew, and I think you had better make an honest woman of me when we get home!"

Smiling, she held her head up for a kiss that would seal their love forever. Against her lips, he whispered, "I'll always love you, and our memories of us here, on our "Island of Dreams!"

EPILOG

Eighteen years later.

It was mid August, and the warm sea breeze drifted across the island to the beach house, where Gail stood in the doorway waiting for Drew, who had the picnic basket.

"Drew, what's keeping you?" inquired Gail, impatiently.

"I'm coming....keep your britches on Darlin!" laughed Drew, as he took one side of the cooler, and started walking toward the bluff. They had bought the beach house some years back from Dr.Philip, and now they spent all their summer and winter vacations there with their family.

As they stood on the bluff, they could hear the children who were now teenagers, playing in the surf below

Dale, who was the oldest at seventeen, spied them coming and began to shout and wave, "Mom! Dad! The water's great!"

Penny, who is fifteen and a beauty at that, started to run toward them to help carry something, "Mom, Dad, the surf 'is terrific! Come on in!" she squealed with delight, as she took the picnic basket from her father. Drew, never realized before just how much his daughter had grown, until now as she stood there in a little yellow bikini,.......and very much a woman. Drew, bent and whispered into Gail's ear, "When did she get to be such a beauty? ......I guess I'll have to keep an eye on her from now on."

"Oh Drew, are you going to be one of those watchful father's?"

By now Philip and Paul, their thirteen year old twins, were running up to them to take the cooler from them "you might know, those two would be here for the food!' laughed Drew, as he shook his head. Later, as they all sat around on the blanket laughing and eating, Drew looked his family over.

Dale, who was dark haired and good looking, loved sports and airplanes, and to others, he was the copy if his Dad.

Penny, was the love of his life. She was blond with dark brown eyes, like her mother's, and she loved life,....and lived it to capacity. Yes.....she was truly becoming a beautiful young lady.

On the other hand.....Philip and Paul, were always into mischief,

Drew, glanced over to where Gail sat, his eyes softened, as he took her in from head to toe. She had gained a few pounds over the years, and a few gray hairs showed here and there, very much like his own. They teased each other about it saying, "There may be snow on the roof.....but there's still fire inside!"

Still she was a mystery to him. She had given him love as a young man,.....and now she had fulfilled his dream of a family. Drew, loved Gail, even more now after all these years. She could still make his blood boil, by looking at him in her special way,.....even now, thinking back over the years, he had an over powering urge to be alone with her, just to make love with this woman that he loved through the years so passionately.

While Gail, packed up the remains of lunch, the children had gone for a walk up the beach, and were now almost out of sight, when Drew reached over and took her hand in his, and as she looked up at him with a smile, and a certain look in her eye, he bent and kissed her. While still holding her close, he whispered, "The kid's are gone, let's go up to the house?"

"Oh Drew, I thought you'de never ask!?" He, could hear her laughing, as she raced ahead of him toward the house.

Later, lying back on the bed, with only the sheet over them, Gail rested her head on his shoulder, saying softly, "It's still wonderful after all these years. You my Darling just get better and better." Drew laughed, as he held her a little closer and kissed the top of her head.

"Ya Sweetheart, all my dreams have come true, just loving and being near you......especially here... in our home, on our Island of Dreams!"

About the Author

Norma Marie was born in Newton, Massachusetts, where at an early age she began to tell stories to all that would listen.

Many stories were written in the evening after the children were in bed. One story that was written on school paper was put away with some odd papers.

Many years later, her daughter found these papers. Since then, she has written for her own enjoyment and now she writes for all that love to read.

Norma writes with true feelings and facts of life that come with maturity.

This book, *Island of Dreams*, is a product of her love for writing.

She now lives in Maine with her husband, Dennis, who she has been married to for fifty-five years.

Printed in the United States
725000003B